An Apprenticeship

ALSO BY CLARICE LISPECTOR

AVAILABLE FROM NEW DIRECTIONS

AN APPRENTICESHIP
OR THE BOOK OF
PLEASURES

Clarice Lispector

Translated from the Portuguese by Stefan Tobler

Afterword by Sheila Heti

Edited by Benjamin Moser

A NEW DIRECTIONS BOOK

Originally published as *Uma aprendizagem ou o livro dos prazeres.*
Published by arrangement with the Heirs of Clarice Lispector and Agencia Literaria
Carmen Balcells, Barcelona

 BIBLIOTECA NACIONAL   MINISTÉRIO DO
TURISMO

Obra publicada com o apoio do Ministério da Cidadania do Brasil | Fundação
Biblioteca Nacional em cooperação com o Ministério das Relações Exteriores
*Published with the support of the Brazilian Ministry of Citizenship | National
Library Foundation in cooperation with the Ministry of Foreign Affairs*

First published in cloth by New Directions in 2021 and in paper as NDP1533 in 2022
Manufactured in the United States of America
Design by Erik Rieselbach

Library of Congress Cataloging-in-Publication Data
Names: Lispector, Clarice, author. | Tobler, Stefan, 1974– translator. |
Heti, Sheila, 1976– writer of afterword. | Moser, Benjamin, editor.
Title: An apprenticeship, or, The book of pleasures / Clarice Lispector ;
translated from the Portuguese by Stefan Tobler ; afterword by Sheila Heti ;
edited by Benjamin Moser.
Other titles: Aprendizagem. English | Book of pleasures
Description: First edition. | New York : New Directions, 2021.
Identifiers: LCCN 2020043515 | ISBN 9780811230612 (hardcover) |
ISBN 9780811230674 (ebook)
Subjects: LCSH: Man-woman relationships—Fiction. | Psychological fiction.
Classification: LCC PQ9697.L585 A8713 2021 | DDC 869.3/42—dc23
LC record available at https://lccn.loc.gov/2020043515

10 9 8 7 6 5 4 3 2 1

New Directions Books are published for James Laughlin
by New Directions Publishing Corporation
80 Eighth Avenue, New York 10011

*After this I looked, and, behold, a door was opened in heaven: and
the first voice which I heard was as it were of a trumpet talking
with me; which said, Come up hither, and I will shew thee things
which must be hereafter.*

—Revelation 4:1

I prove ....
That the highest expression of pain ....
Consists in its essence of happiness ....

—Augusto dos Anjos

Jeanne:
Je ne veux pas mourir! J'ai peur!
...
Il y a la joie qui est la plus forte!

—Paul Claudel, from his libretto
for Arthur Honegger's oratorio
Jeanne d'Arc au bûcher

Contents

Note

THIS BOOK DEMANDED A GREATER LIBERTY THAT I WAS afraid to give. It is far above me. Humbly I tried to write it. I am stronger than I.

C.L.

THE ORIGIN OF SPRING
OR
THE NECESSARY DEATH
IN THE MIDDLE OF THE DAY

, being so busy, she'd just come from the grocery shopping that the maid had rushed because she was shirking more every day, though she only came in to get lunch and dinner ready, she'd dealt with a few things on the phone, including one awfully difficult call to the plumber, she'd gone to the kitchen to put away the groceries and place the apples, which were her best food, in the fruit bowl, despite not knowing how to arrange fruit, but Ulisses had hinted at the future possibility of for example making the fruit bowl look pretty, saw what the maid had left for dinner before leaving, because lunch had been terrible, meanwhile she'd noticed that the small terrace which was a perk of her ground-floor apartment needed to be washed, got a call inviting her to a charity cocktail party for something she hadn't quite understood but which was related to her primary school, thank God it was the holidays, gone to her wardrobe to choose a dress that would make her extremely attractive for the meeting with Ulisses who'd already said that she had no fashion sense, remembered that as it was Saturday he'd have more time because he wasn't teaching at the University's summer school on Saturdays, thought about what he was becoming for her, about what he seemed to want her to know, supposed that he was just wanting her to live without pain, he'd once said that he wanted, when someone asked her name, for her not to say "Lóri" but to be able to reply "my name is I," since your name, he'd said, is an I, wondered if the black-and-white dress would do,

then from the very womb, like a distant quivering in the earth that hardly knew itself to be a sign of the earthquake, from the uterus, from the tensed heart came the gigantic tremor of a powerful, shaking pain, from the whole body a shaking—and with subtle grimaces of face and of body at last with the difficulty of an oil ripping open the ground—came at last the great dry sob, a wordless sob without any sound even for herself, the one she hadn't suspected, the one she'd never wanted and hadn't foreseen—rattled like the strong tree that is more deeply shaken than the fragile tree—at last pipes and veins were burst, then

she sat down to rest and was soon pretending that she was a blue woman because the dusk later on might be blue, pretends she's spinning sensations with threads of gold, pretends that childhood is today and silver-plated with toys, pretends that a vein hadn't opened and pretends that from it in whitest silence scarlet blood isn't pouring, and that she isn't pale as death but this she was pretending as if it really were true, amidst the pretending she needed to speak the truth of an opaque stone so it could contrast with the glinting green pretending, pretends that she loves and is loved, pretends that she doesn't need to die of longing, pretends that she's lying in the transparent palm of the hand of God, not Lóri but her secret name that for the time being she still can't enjoy, pretends she's alive and not dying since in the end living was no more than getting ever closer to death, pretends she doesn't drop her arms in confusion when the threads of gold she's been spinning get tangled and she doesn't know how to undo the fine cold thread, pretends she's clever enough to undo the knots of ship's rope that were binding her wrists, pretends she has a basket of pearls just in order to look at the color of the moon since she is lunar, pretends that she closes her eyes and beloved beings appear when she opens her eyes moist with gratitude, pretends that everything she has isn't pretend, pretends that her chest is relaxing and a weightless golden light is guiding her through a forest of silent pools and tranquil mortalities, pretends she isn't lunar, pretends she isn't crying inside

—because gently now, though her eyes were dry, her heart was soaked; she'd now escaped the voracity of living. She remembered to write Ulisses to tell him what had happened,

but nothing had happened that was utterable in written or spoken words, the system Ulisses had invented was good: whatever she didn't know or couldn't say, she'd write down and mutely give him the piece of paper—but this time she didn't even have anything to tell.

Lucid and calm now, Lóri remembered reading that a captive animal's hysterical movements were intended to free it, through one of these movements, from the unknown thing that was holding it—not knowing which single, exact, and liberating movement was what made an animal hysterical: it was pleading for a loss of control—during Lóri's wise loss of control she'd grasped for herself now the liberating advantages of her more primitive and animal life: she had pleaded hysterically to so many contradictory and violent feelings that the liberating feeling had finally released her from the net, in her animal ignorance she didn't even know how,

she was worn out by the effort of the liberated animal.

And now the moment had come to decide whether she'd keep seeing Ulisses. In sudden rebellion she didn't want to learn what he was patiently seeming to want to teach and she herself to learn—she was rebelling more than everything because it wasn't for her the right time for "meditation" which suddenly seemed ridiculous: she was quivering with pure desire as she did before and after menstruation. But it was as if he wanted her to learn to walk on her own legs and only then, prepared for freedom by Ulisses, would she be his—what did he want from her, other than to desire her contentedly? At first Lóri had been wrong and thought that Ulisses wanted to transmit to her some things from his philosophy classes but he said: "philosophy's not what you need, if it was it would be easy: you'd audit my classes and I'd talk with you in other terms,"

well now that the earthquake would lend itself to her hysteria and now that she was liberated she could even put off the decision not to see Ulisses: except she wanted to see him today and, though she couldn't stand his mute desire, she knew that in fact she was the one provoking him in order to try to break the patience with which he was waiting; she used the allowance her father sent her to buy expensive, always tight dresses, it was the only way she knew to attract him and

it was time to get dressed: she looked in the mirror and was only beautiful because she was a woman: her body was slim and strong, one of the—imaginary—reasons that made Ulisses desire her; she chose, despite the heat, a dress made of thick cloth, almost shapeless, her body would be the shape but

dressing up was a ritual that put her in a serious mood: the cloth was no longer a mere fabric, it was becoming the matter of the thing and it was this material to which with her body she gave body—how could a simple rag gain such movement? her hair, washed and dried by the sun that morning on the little terrace was of the oldest chestnut silk—beautiful? no, a woman: Lóri then carefully painted her lips and eyes, which she did, according to a colleague, very badly, dabbed perfume on her forehead and cleavage—the earth was perfumed with a thousand crushed leaves and flowers: Lóri put on perfume and this was one of her imitations of the world, she who was trying so hard to learn life—with perfume, somehow she was intensifying what she was and that's why she couldn't use perfumes that contradicted her: perfuming herself was an instinctive knowledge, come from millennia of apparently passive women learning, and, like any art, it demanded a minimum of self-knowledge: she'd wear a slightly suffocating perfume, delicious as soil, as if her resting head were crushing the soil, and whose name she wouldn't say to any of her fellow teachers: because it was hers, it was her, since for Lóri putting on perfume was a secret and almost religious act

—should she wear earrings? she hesitated, for she wanted simply delicate and unadorned ears, something modestly nude, she hesitated again: even richer would be to hide her doe-like ears behind her hair and make a secret of them, but she couldn't resist: she uncovered them, tucking her hair behind her incongruous and pale ears: an Egyptian queen? no, all adorned like the women of the Bible, and there was also something about her made-up eyes that said with melancholy: decipher me, my love, or I'll have to devour you, and

now ready, dressed, as pretty as she could make herself, she again wondered whether or not to meet Ulisses—ready, arms hanging by her side, lost in thought, would she or wouldn't she meet him? around Ulisses she acted like the virgin she no longer was, though she was sure he sensed it too, that strange wise man who nonetheless didn't seem to guess that she wanted love.

Once more, in her confused hesitation, what reassured her was something that had so often calmed and supported her:

the knowledge that everything that exists, exists with absolute exactness and ultimately whatever she ended up doing or not doing would not escape that exactness; something the size of a pinhead would not extend by a fraction of a millimeter beyond the size of a pinhead: everything that existed was of a great perfection. Except most of what existed with such perfection was, technically, invisible: the truth, clear and exact in itself, was vague and almost imperceptible upon reaching the woman.

Well, she sighed, even if it wasn't reaching me clearly, at least she knew that there was a secret meaning to the things of life. So it was she knew that she occasionally, even if somewhat confusedly, ended up sensing perfection—

these thoughts again, which she was somehow using as a reminder (that, because of the perfection that existed, she'd end up doing the right thing)—once again the reminder acted upon her and with eyes darkened even more now with her perturbed thoughts, she decided she'd see Ulisses at least one more time.

And it wasn't because he was waiting for her, since often Lóri, counting on Ulisses's offensively excessive patience, just wouldn't show up, without letting him know; though at the idea that Ulisses's patience could run out, her hand rose to her throat trying to staunch an anguish like the one she felt when she wondered "who am I? who is Ulisses? who are people?" It was as if Ulisses had an answer for all of this and had decided not to give it—and now the anguish was returning because she was realizing once again that she did need Ulisses, which made her despair—she wanted to be able to keep seeing him, but without needing him so violently. If she were a person entirely alone, as before, she'd know how to feel and act inside a system. But now, with Ulisses entering ever more fully into her life, she, feeling protected by him, had started to fear losing his protection—

—though she herself wasn't sure what she meant by "being protected": did she, perhaps, have a childish wish to have everything but without the anxiety of having to give something in return? Was protection a presence? If she were protected by Ulisses even more than she already was, she'd immediately aim for the maximum: to be so protected that she wouldn't fear being free: since from her flights of freedom she'd always have somewhere to return.

Having glimpsed her whole body in the mirror, she thought that protection would also mean no longer being one single body: being one single body would give her, as it did now, the impression of being cut off from herself. Having a single body surrounded by isolation, made that body so circumscribed, she felt, that she'd then fear being a person on her own, she looked greedily at herself in the mirror and said amazed: how mysterious I am, I'm so delicate and strong, and the lips' curve maintained its innocence.

It then seemed to her, mulling things over, that there wasn't a man or woman who hadn't chanced to look in the mirror and been taken aback. For a fraction of a second the person saw herself as an object to be looked at, which could be called narcissism but, already influenced by Ulisses, she'd call: pleasure in being. To find in the external figure the echoes of the internal figure: ah, so it's true I wasn't just imagining it: I exist.

And because of that very fact of having seen herself in the mirror, she felt how small her condition was because a body is smaller than the thought—to the point that it would be useless to have more freedom: her small condition wouldn't allow her to make use of freedom. Whereas the condition of the Universe was so great that it wasn't called a condition. Ulisses's human condition was greater than hers which, nonetheless, was rich in day-to-day life. But her mismatch with the world was so great it was comic: she hadn't managed to walk in step with the things around her. She'd already tried to keep pace with the world and had only made a fool of herself: one of her legs was always far too short. (The paradox was that she ought to accept her limping condition gladly, because it too was part of her condition.) (Only when she tried to keep up with the world did she shatter and frighten herself.) And suddenly she smiled to herself with a bitter smile, but that wasn't bad because it too belonged to her condition. (Lóri often grew tired because she never stopped being.)

It seemed to her that Ulisses, if she plucked up the courage to tell him what she was feeling, and she never would, if she told him he'd reply more or less like this and very calmly: the condition can't be cured but the fear of the condition is curable. He'd say that or something else—it irritated her because every time a sharper or wiser thought like this occurred to her, she'd suppose that Ulisses was the one who'd have it,

she, who recognized with gratitude the general superiority of men who smelled like men and not perfume, and recognized with irritation that in truth these thoughts she was calling sharp or wise were themselves the result of spending more time with Ulisses. And even the fact that her "sufferings" now came less frequently, which she owed to Ulisses—"sufferings"? was being pain? And was it only when being was no longer pain that Ulisses would consider she was ready to sleep with him? No, I won't go, she then thought to shake loose of him. But this time she didn't want him to go to the bar and wait for her: to offend him she wanted to tell him she wasn't going, he who was used to her not showing up and not even letting him know. This time she'd tell him she wasn't going, which was a more positive offense.

HAD MOMENTS GONE BY OR THREE THOUSAND YEARS? Moments according to the clock by which time is divided, three thousand years according to what Lóri felt when with heavy anguish, all dressed and made up, she reached the window. She was a four-millennia-old woman.

No—it wasn't red. It was the sensual union of the day with its duskiest hour. It was almost night and there it was still light. If only there was red visibly, the way it was inside her intrinsically. But it was a heat of light without color, and motionless. No, the woman couldn't breathe. She was dry and limpid. And outside the only birds that were flying had taxidermied feathers. If the woman would close her eyes in order not to see the heat, for it was a visible heat, only then would the slow hallucination appear symbolizing it: she was seeing thick elephants approach, sweet and heavy elephants, their skin dry, though soaked inside their flesh by an unbearable hot tenderness; they had trouble bearing themselves, which made them slow and heavy.

It was still too early to turn on the lights, which at least would hasten the night. The night that wouldn't, and wouldn't, and wouldn't come, that was impossible. And her love that now was impossible—that was dry the way the fever of someone who doesn't sweat was love without opium or morphine. And "I love you" was a splinter you couldn't remove with tweezers. A splinter buried in the toughest part of the sole of your foot.

Ah, and the lack of thirst. Heat with thirst would be bearable. But ah, the lack of thirst. There was nothing but lacks and absences. And not even will. Just splinters with no protruding ends by which to pluck and expel them. Only the teeth were moist. Inside a voracious and parched mouth the moist but hard teeth—and especially the mouth voracious for nothingness. And the nothingness was hot on that late afternoon eternalized by the planet Mars.

Her eyes open and diamond. On the roofs the dry sparrows. "I love you, people," was an impossible phrase. Humanity for her was like eternal death that nevertheless hadn't had the relief of finally dying. Nothing, nothing was dying on that parched afternoon, nothing rotting. And at six o'clock it was like noon. It was noon with a watchful noise from a water pump's motor, a pump that had been working for so long without water and that had become rusted iron: for two days there had been no water in different parts of the city. Nothing had ever been as awake as her body without sweat and her diamond eyes, with all vibration stilled. And the God? No. Not even the anguish. Her chest empty, not contracted. There was no scream.

Meanwhile it was summer. An expansive summer like the empty playground during school holidays. Pain? None. No sign of a tear and no sweat. No salt. Just a heavy sweetness: like that of the slow hides of the elephants made of dried-out leather. The limpid and hot squalor. Think about her man? No, that was the splinter in the heart-bit of the foot again. Regret not having married and not having children? Fifteen children hung on her, without swinging in the absence of wind. Ah, if only her hands would start growing moist. Even if there were water, out of hatred she wouldn't wash. It was out of hatred that there wasn't water. Nothing was flowing. The difficulty was a motionless thing. It's a diamond jewel. The cicada with its dry throat wouldn't stop growling. And what if the God finally liquefies into rain? No. I don't even want that. Out of calm dry hatred, this is what I want, this silence made of heat that the tough cicada makes you feel. Feel? There's nothing to feel. Except this hard lack of the opium that soothes. I want this intolerable thing to keep going because I want eternity. I want this ongoing waiting like the red song of the cicada, because all this is the halted death, it's the Eternity of trillions of years of stars and of the Earth, it's rutting without desire, dogs without barking. It's at this time that good and evil don't exist. It's the sudden forgiveness, we who nourish ourselves with the secret pleasure of punishment. Now it's the indifference to forgiveness. For there is no more judgment. It's not a forgiveness that comes after a judgment. It's the absence of judge and felon. And it's not raining, not raining. Menstruation doesn't exist. The ovaries are two dry pearls. I'll speak the truth to you: out of dry hatred, that's exactly what I want, and for it not to rain.

And just then she hears something. A thing dry too that leaves her even drier of attention. It's a roll of dry thunder, without a drop of saliva, that rolls, but where to? In the naked and absolutely blue sky there's not a cloud of love crying. The thunder must be very far away. At the same time the air has a sugary scent of big elephants, and of sugary jasmine from the house next door. India invading Rio de Janeiro with its sugary women. A scent of cemetery carnations. Would everything change so quickly? For someone who had neither night nor rain nor rotting of wood in water—for someone who had nothing but pearls, would night really fall? Would there be wood rotting at last, carnations living off rain in the cemetery, rain that comes from Malaysia?

The urgency is still motionless but already has a trembling inside it. Lóri doesn't realize that the trembling is her own, as she hadn't realized that what was burning her wasn't the hot dusk, and instead her own human heat. She only realizes that now some thing will change, that it will rain or night will fall. But she can't bear the wait for a change, and before the rain falls, the diamond of her eyes liquefies into two tears.

And at last the sky softens.

LÓRI CALLED HIS NUMBER:

—I can't come, Ulisses, I'm not well.

There was a pause. He finally asked:

—Physically not well?

She answered that it was nothing physical. Then he said:

—Lóri, said Ulisses, and suddenly he seemed serious though he was speaking calmly, Lóri: one of the things I've learned is that we ought to live despite. Despite, we should eat. Despite, we should love. Despite, we should die. It's even often this despite that spurs us on. The despite was what gave me an anguish that when unsatisfied was the creator of my own life. It was despite that I stopped on the street and stood looking at you while you were waiting for a taxi. And immediately desiring you, that body of yours that isn't even pretty, but it's the body I want. But I want it all, including the soul. That's why it doesn't matter that you're not coming, I'll wait as long as I have to.

—Why didn't you ever marry? she asked out of the blue.

—Because—and his voice was the voice of someone smiling—because I never felt the need to and luckily I had the women I wanted.

She said goodbye, bowed her head with modesty and joy. For despite, she'd had joy. He'd wait for her, she knew that now. Until she learned.

Everything was calm now. And as she remembered her own Biblical image, as she'd looked in the mirror before, she found it so somehow lovely, that she had to give this aspect of beauty to someone. And that someone could only be Ulisses who knew how to see the disguised and innermost beauty that a common person couldn't. But he, at a glance, could. He was a man, she was a woman, and a miracle more extraordinary than this could only be compared to the falling star that crosses the black sky almost imaginarily and leaves as its trail the vivid amazement of a living Universe. He was a man and she was a woman.

She who had so often reached the point of hating Ulisses, even while still getting him to want her.

Ah! she screamed suddenly mute, may the God help me achieve the impossible, only the impossible matters to me!

She didn't even understand what she meant by this, but as if she had been heard in her greatest human plea and somehow, just by wanting it, had touched the impossible, she said quietly, audibly, humbly: thank you.

Through her grave defects—which she might one day be able to mention without boasting—she had now come to be able to love. Even that glorification: she loved the Nothing. The awareness of her permanent human fall was leading her to the love of the Nothing. And those falls—like those of Christ who fell several times beneath the weight of the cross—and those falls were what were starting to make her life. Maybe it was her "despites" that, Ulisses had said, despites full of anguish and lack of understanding of herself, were leading her to build bit by bit a life. With stones of poor material she might have been building the horror, and accepting the mystery of with horror loving the unknown God. She didn't know what to do with herself, already born, except this: Thou, the God, whom I love like one falling into the nothing.

After that it was easy to call Ulisses and tell him she'd changed her mind and he could wait for her in the bar. What she was doing to herself was cruel: taking advantage of her raw living flesh in order to get to know herself better, since the wound was open. But it hurt too much to head in that direction. So she preferred to calm down and decided that, in the taxi, she'd think about Ulisses's straight nose, his face marked by the slow apprenticeship of life, his lips that she'd never kissed.

Except she didn't want to go empty-handed. And as if she were bringing him a flower, she wrote on a piece of paper some words that would give him pleasure: "There's a being who lives inside me as if it were his house, and it is. It's a black and shiny horse that despite being completely wild—for it never lived in anyone before nor has anyone ever bridled and saddled it—despite being completely wild it has for precisely that reason the primal sweetness of someone who is not afraid: sometimes it eats from my hand. Its muzzle is moist and fresh. I kiss its muzzle. When I die, the black horse will lose its home and suffer a lot. Unless he chooses another house and that other house isn't afraid of something at the same time wild and tender. I should mention that he has no name: just call him and you'll get his name right. Or not, but, once he's been called with sweetness and authority, he'll come. If he sniffs and feels that a house-body is free, he'll trot without a sound and come. I should also say that you shouldn't fear his whinnying: people make the mistake of thinking they're the ones whinnying with pleasure or rage, people take fright at the excess of sweetness which this is for the first time."

She smiled. Ulisses would like it, he'd think she was the horse. Was she?

AS IF A HERD OF TRANSPARENT GAZELLES WERE PASS-
ing through the air of the world at dusk—that's what Lóri
managed some weeks later. The translucid victory was as light
and promising as pre-sexual pleasure.

She'd become more skillful: as if slowly getting used to the
Earth, the Moon, the Sun, and strangely to Mars most of all.
She was on a terrestrial platform from which for split seconds
she seemed to see the super-reality of what is truly real. More
real—Ulisses said to her when she in her own way told him
about the almost non-event—more real than reality.

The next day she patiently tried dusk again. She was waiting. With her senses sharpened by the world that surrounded
her as if she were entering Venus's unknown lands. Nothing
happened.

LUMINESCENCE . . .

FROM ULISSES SHE'D LEARNED TO HAVE THE COURAGE to have faith—lots of courage, faith in what? In faith itself, since faith can be a real scare, it can mean falling into the abyss, Lóri was afraid of falling into the abyss and was holding on to one of Ulisses's hands while Ulisses's other hand was pushing her into the abyss—soon she'd have to let go of the hand that was weaker than the one pushing her, and fall, life isn't a joke because in the middle of the day you die.

A human being's most pressing need was to become a human being.

AND THERE WAS THE NIGHT OF TERROR. SHE KEPT hearing footsteps coming and going. She peeked out of a gap between the blinds and saw it was the same half-crazed man, with long monkey arms, who'd followed her that day. His slow steps were coming and going and returning. Lóri knew he was waiting for her. Through the blinds she saw that he was smoking and patiently walking back and forth.

She couldn't bear it any longer and called Ulisses. He said he'd be there in minutes. Minutes or interminable hours? Had his car's brake cable broken or something like that?

Finally she heard his car stop. From the window she saw the two men talking, and a calm whisper that was carrying on too long.

At last she saw the man go away, at the same time that Ulisses was saying to her in a low voice:

—Lóri, it's fine. It was a man you looked at quite a bit today, maybe you didn't realize, and he followed you hopefully, hoping you'd open the door.

—Come to the door.

He came:

—Would you like a coffee? She asked as a pretext to get him to come in.

He stayed on the threshold. She was standing, in a short and transparent nightdress. He was going to say: "you can sleep easy now, I found a way to get him to go." But before he said that he stopped short, his lips pursed, and looked her up and down. Finally he said:

—I'll call in the morning.

With the despair of a woman scorned, she heard his car pull away.

Ulisses's gaze robbed her of sleep. She looked herself all over in the mirror in order to figure out what Ulisses had seen. And she found herself attractive. Yet he hadn't wanted to come in.

She waited unhurriedly for dawn. The best light for living was at dawn, faint such a faint promise of early morning. She knew that, had experienced it countless times. Like a painter who seeks the light most suited to him, Lóri preferred for the discovery of what's called living those shy hours at the vague start of the day. At dawn she'd step onto her little terrace and if she was lucky it would be dawn with a full moon. She'd learned all this through Ulisses. In the past she'd avoided feeling. She still did but now with short incursions into life.

But she didn't fear the moon because she was more lunar than solar and could see with wide-open eyes in the dark dawns the sinister moon in the sky. So she bathed all over in the lunar rays, as there are others who sunbathed. And was becoming profoundly limpid.

In this cool dawn she went to the terrace and reflecting a bit came to the frightening certainty that her thoughts were as supernatural as a story that takes place after death. She had simply felt, suddenly, that thinking wasn't natural for her. After that she'd reached the conclusion that she didn't have a day-to-day but a life-to-life. And that life that was hers in the dawns was supernatural with its countless moons bathing her in such a terrible silver liquid.

More than anything she'd now learned to approach things without linking them to their function. It now seemed she could see how things and people would be before we gave them the meaning of our human hope or our pain. If there were no humans on earth, it would be like this: it would rain, things would get drenched, alone, and would dry and then burn drily under the sun and get toasted in the dust. Without giving the world our meaning, how frightened Lóri was! She was scared of the rain when she separated it from the city and the open umbrellas and the fields soaking up the water. Then the thing she called death would attract her so strongly that she could only call bravery the way in which, out of solidarity and pity for others, she was still bound to what she called life. It would be profoundly amoral not to wait for death as all others wait for that final hour. It would have been sneaky of her to leap ahead in time, and unforgivable to be cleverer than others. For that reason, despite her intense curiosity about death, Lóri was waiting.

Morning broke.

Whatever had happened in Lóri's thought in that dawn was as inexpressible and incommunicable as the voice of a hushed human being. Only the silence of a mountain was comparable. The silence of Switzerland, for example. She remembered fondly the time when her father was rich and they'd travel for several months a year.

As intransmissible as humans were, they were always trying to communicate with gestures, with stutters, with badly said words and bad words. Morning was already well underway when she made strong coffee, drank it and got ready to communicate with Ulisses, since Ulisses was her man. She wrote:

"Night is so vast in the mountains. So uninhabited. The Spanish night has the scent and the hard echo of the tap dance, the Italian night has the warm sea even in its absence. But the night of Bern has the silence.

"We can try in vain to read so as not to hear it, to think quickly so as to disguise it, to invent a plan, a fragile bridge that barely connects us to the suddenly improbable next day. How to get beyond the peace that lies in wait for us. Mountains so high that despair becomes bashful. The ears prick, the head bends, the whole body listens: not a sound. No possible rooster. How to be within reach of that profound meditation of silence? Of this silence without memory of words. If thou art death, how to bless thee?

"It's a silence, Ulisses, that doesn't sleep: it's insomniac: immobile but insomniac and without ghosts. It's terrible—not a single ghost. It's useless to want to populate it with the possibility of a door that opens with a creak, of a curtain that opens and 'says' something. It's empty and without promise. Like me, Ulisses? If at least there were wind. Wind is rage, rage is life. But during the nights I spent in Bern there was no wind and every leaf was inlaid on the branch of the immobile trees. Or it was the time of year for snow. Which is silent but leaves a trace—everything turns white, children laugh playing with the flakes, footsteps creak and leave prints. This is so intense during the day that the night is inhabited still. There's a continuity that is life. But this silence doesn't leave evidence. You can't speak of silence the way you speak of snow. Silence is the profound secret night of the world. And you can't speak of silence the way you speak of snow: have you felt the silence of those nights? No one who has heard tells. There's a freemasonry around the silence that consists of not speaking of it and of worshipping it without words.

"Night falls, Ulisses, with the little joys of someone turning on the lights, with the fatigue that does so much to justify the day. The children of Bern fall asleep, the last doors are closed. The streets shine on the paving stones and shine already empty. And finally the lights in the houses go out. Just the odd lit streetlight to illuminate the silence.

"But that first silence, Ulisses, is not silence yet. Wait a bit, because the leaves on the trees will adjust their positions, some belated footstep might be heard going hopefully up some stairs.

"But there's a moment in which from the rested body the watchful spirit rises, and from the Earth and the Moon. Then it, the silence, appears. And the heart quickens in recognition: for it is the silence inside us.

"You can quickly think of the day that passed. Or of the friends that passed and were lost forever. But it's no use to try to avoid it: the silence is there. Even the worst suffering, that of lost friendship, is just an attempt to escape. For if at first the silence seems to expect a reply—what an urge, Ulisses, to be called and to respond; soon you discover that it demands nothing of you, perhaps only your silence. But the members of the masonic order know this. How many hours I wasted in the dark supposing that silence judges you—how I waited in vain to be judged by the God. Justifications arise, tragic fabricated justifications, humble apologies to the point of indignity. It's so pleasant for human beings to show at last their indignity and be forgiven with the excuse that humans are humiliated beings from birth.

"Until you discover, Ulisses — it doesn't even want your indignity. It is the Silence. Is it the God?

"You can also try to trick it. Let as if by chance the book on the bedside table fall to the floor. But — horror — the book falls into the silence and gets lost in its mute and motionless whirl. And what if a crazed bird were to sing? Vain hope. The song would just cross the silence like a light flute. The thing that most resembled, in the realm of sound, the silence, was a flute.

"So, if you dare, you stop fighting. Do you enter it, go into it to Hell? You go with it, we the only ghosts of a night in Bern. Enter. Don't wait out the rest of the darkness before it, just the silence itself. It will be as if we were in a ship so uncommonly enormous that we didn't realize we were in a ship. And as if it were sailing so slowly that we didn't realize we were moving. A man can't do more than this. Living on the edge of death and of the stars is a tenser vibration than the veins can stand. There's not even a son of a star and a woman as a merciful intermediary. The heart must present itself alone to the Nothing and alone beat out in silence its palpitations in the shadows. You only sense your own heart in your ears. When it presents itself completely naked, it's not even communication, it's submission. For we were only made for the little silence, not for the silence of the stars.

"And if you don't dare, don't enter. Wait out the rest of the darkness before the silence, only your feet wet from the surf of something that spreads out inside us. Wait. One insoluble in the other. One beside the other, two things that do not see one another in the darkness. Wait. Not for the end of silence but for the blessed help of a third element: the light of dawn.

"Afterward you never again forget it, Ulisses. There's no point even in fleeing to another city. For when you least expect it you'll recognize it—suddenly. While crossing the street amidst the beeping of horns. Between one ghostly cackle and another. After an uttered word. Sometimes in the very heart of a word you recognize the Silence. The ears are spooked, the gaze goes blank—there it is. And this time it's a ghost."

Writing brought her relief. She had bags under her eyes after the sleepless night, was tired, but for an instant—ah how Ulisses would want to know—happy. Because, if she hadn't expressed the inexpressible silence, she'd spoken like a monkey who grunts and makes incoherent gestures, transmitting who knows what. Lóri was. What? But she was.

WHAT WAS REALLY HAPPENING WITH LÓRI WAS THAT, due to a decision so deep that the reasons for it escaped her— she had out of fear cut out pain. Only with Ulisses had she come to learn that you can't cut out pain—otherwise you'd suffer all the time. And she had cut it out without even having some other thing that in itself could stand in for the vision of things through the pain of existence, as before. Without pain, she'd been left with nothing, lost in her own world and in the wider world without any connection to people.

It was then that Ulisses had turned up in her life. He, who had been interested in Lóri only because of desire, was now seeming to see how out of reach she was. And more than that: not just out of reach for him but for herself and for the world. She was living off a tightness in her chest: life.

That's when their meetings had begun: she only seemed to want to learn something from him and had deceived herself thinking she wanted to learn because he was a professor of Philosophy, using him in that hope. When the hope died, upon seeing that he hadn't the slightest intention of teaching her a "philosophical" or "literary" way to live, it was already too late: she was bound to him because she wanted to be desired, above all she liked to be desired rather savagely when he'd drink too much. She'd already been desired by other men but what was new was Ulisses wanting her and waiting with patience—even when he was drunk, which didn't make him lose control—and waiting with patience for her to be ready, while he would say of himself that he was in the middle of his apprenticeship, but so far beyond her that she was transforming into a tiny body, empty and in pain, just that. And she was longing for him exactly because he seemed to her like the border between the past and whatever was to come—whatever would come? Nothing, she'd think in despair. She was waiting, since she had nothing to do except teach in a primary school in the mornings or otherwise be on holiday as she was now, read a little, eat and sleep, and meet Ulisses who was barely transforming her, or if he was transforming her then not enough. And wait.

Yet it was her dread of a possible soul intimacy with Ulisses that made her annoyed with him. Was she in fact fighting her own intense urge to come closer to the impossible part of another human being? Ah, if only the pain were no longer there, and she were helping Ulisses by quickly applying herself to learning—what?—out of fear that in the end he would think it was now too late for her and gently draw back. It seemed to her nonetheless that she herself was getting in the way of their joint mission. Because though she didn't know what she wanted, besides sleeping with him someday, she guessed that it was something so difficult to give and receive that he might draw back.

Lóri herself had a kind of dread of going, as if she could go too far—in what direction? Which was making it hard to go.

She kept holding back a little as if holding the reins of a horse that could gallop off and take her God knows where. She was saving herself. Why and for what? What was she sparing herself for? There was a certain fear of her own capability, large or small, maybe because she didn't know her own limits. Were the limits of a human divine? They were. But it kept seeming to her that, as a woman sometimes saved herself untouched in order to give herself one day to love, she might want to die still completely whole so that eternity would have all of her.

Did she want salvation? Pain had become stiffened and paralyzed inside her chest, as if she no longer wanted to use it as a way of living. But this precaution—that had come after Ulisses—was not yet the one that would save her: for instead of pain, nothing had come except a stop to the life of feelings. If salvation was what she was hoping for from Ulisses, would that be asking so much and so big that he'd decline? She'd never seen anyone save someone else, so she was afraid of an approach that would only disillusion her by confirming that one being cannot encroach on another the way shadows trespass on each other.

Sometimes she'd regress and succumb to a total irresponsibility: the desire to be possessed by Ulisses without binding herself to him, as she'd done with the others. But therein too she might fail: she was now a big-city woman but the danger was the strong rural heritage in her blood from way back. And she knew that this heritage could make her suddenly want more, telling herself: no, I don't want to be just me, because I have my own I, what I want is the extreme connection between me and the sandy and perfumed earth. What she called earth had already become the synonym for Ulisses, so much did she want her ancestors' earth. With the children she taught in the mornings, she hadn't managed to become one with the earth, as if she weren't ready to have the connection of a woman with whatever might represent sons and daughters. And there remained, still as a shadow of the dark pain of which she'd been made before Ulisses, the disheartening thought: whatever she was, was only a small part of herself.

Her immeasurable soul. For she was the World. And yet she was living so little. This was one of the sources of her humility and forced acceptance, and also kept her weak in the face of any possibility of action.

Moreover feeling overly humble was paradoxically where her haughtiness came from. For her haughtiness—which was reflected in her supple and calm way of walking—her haughtiness came from the obscure certainty that her roots were strong, and that her humility was not just human humility: for every root is strong, and her humility came from the obscure certainty that all roots are humble, earthy and full of a moist vigor in their gnarled rooted modesty.

Of course none of this was thought: it was lived, with the odd rapid sweeping beam in the night illuminating the sky for a fraction of a second of thought in the dark.

What had also saved Lóri was that she was feeling that if her own world weren't human, there would still be room for her, and with great beauty: she'd be a smudge of instincts, affections and ferocities, a shimmering irradiation of peace and struggle, the way she was humanly, but it would be permanent: because if her world weren't human she'd be a creature. For an instant then she scorned whatever was human and experienced the silent soul of animal life.

And it was good. "Not understanding" was so vast that it surpassed all understanding—understanding was always limited. But not-understanding had no frontiers and led to the infinite, to the God. It wasn't a not-understanding like that of a simpleton. What was good was having an intelligence and not understanding. It was a strange blessing like that of having madness without being crazy. It was a gentle disinterest toward the so-called matters of the intellect, a sweetness of stupidity.

But sometimes the unbearable anxiety would come: she wanted to understand enough so that she'd at least become more aware of everything she didn't understand. Though deep down she didn't want to comprehend. She knew it was impossible and every time she had thought she'd understood herself it was because she'd understood wrongly. Understanding was always a mistake—she preferred the largesse, so wide and free and without mistakes, of not-understanding. It was bad, but at least you knew you were in the full human condition.

Yet sometimes she'd guess right. There were cosmic streaks that substituted for understanding.

LÓRI HAD ALREADY TOLD ULISSES ABOUT THE PERIOD, in Campos, when her parents were rich and would travel, staying in this country or that for months with their children, until, at the same time as her mother died, the family fortune was reduced to a third. Ulisses, despite only ever having traveled inside Brazil, had never asked her touristy questions. Nor did she ever describe places. Lóri had barely spoken of herself in other countries. She'd said little but he, through the attention he'd given her, seemed to have heard more than she'd told him.

She'd spoken of Paris but not of the land called Paris. She'd spoken of how the winter there was full of darkness at dusk and how it snowed bad snow, not the light kind but the thick kind, and even more: the frozen flakes borne on gusts of wind lashed her face already stiff with cold. She'd mentioned that one day, as it got dark, she'd started to cry quietly on a street corner. There was no one around, and so she'd started to talk to herself: "O God help me in this frozen darkness that is my own."

—On that corner, she'd said to Ulisses in the same quiet voice, I felt lost, saved from some shipwreck and thrown onto a dark, cold, deserted beach.

Paris, suddenly, that strange land, had given her the oddest pain—that of her real perdition. Perdition was not the everyday truth but was the unreality that would let her sense her true condition. And everyone else's.

She also told him how that same winter in Paris, she'd gone to a seamstress in a district far from the hotel. Inside she hadn't noticed night fall and, in front of a lit fire, hadn't realized that the cold with the early nightfall had turned freezing. It was the ninth of February. As she went out she was shocked to find it was night. She didn't know the area and there weren't many taxis, those going down that black street already had passengers. She didn't know exactly how far she was from the hotel. She'd stood there waiting in vain for a taxi. And what if she forgot the name of the hotel? And suddenly she no longer had the slightest idea what it was called, such did the names of hotels in all the cities of the world resemble one another and she had lived or just stayed in so many. If she never again remembered the name of the hotel, no one would find her, she'd carry on living in that dirty black district with its blackened buildings, isolated from the rest of Paris and would have to change her life in order to survive. She'd live right there where she'd got lost: it was rare for a person to touch their own perdition. In order to eat would she prostitute herself? Because of the way she was it seemed easier and less distressing than working a shop counter.

She'd lost all sense of how much time she was there that night. It had grown so cold that some men had lit a fire that was the color of intense flames in a barrel on the sidewalk. She too drew close and, like the men, in order not to feel the growing numbness in her freezing feet, she would sometimes stamp her feet imitating them and, again imitating them, rubbing her gloved hands together—until suddenly the unexpected: the empty taxi passing.

She hailed it. And the hotel's name? "Keep going," she said to the driver. "Going where?" he replied grumpy like all Parisian taxi drivers. "Keep going," she replied with feigned sternness. Had she really forgotten the hotel's name? She felt as she had when as a child she'd taken part in plays, and in the wings, before going on stage, she'd shiver with fright because she'd simply forgotten the first lines of what she was supposed to say. Although, once she took to the stage, she'd suddenly talk like a sleepwalker, and only later would gradually become aware of herself and of the audience and manage to perform her role.

It was the taxi's sudden braking, accompanied by the driver's swearing, that gave her the shock she needed and suddenly she remembered the name of the hotel. She said it to the driver and immediately collapsed into a muffled sob of relief and suffering.

Ulisses had listened with a knitted brow. And then said:

—And so you didn't want any more of that. And you stopped the possibility of pain, which no one gets away with. You just stopped and found nothing beyond it. I'm not saying I have much, but I still have intense searching and violent hope. Not that quiet and sweet voice of yours. And I don't cry, if I need to one day I'll scream, Lóri. I'm in the middle of a struggle and much closer to whatever people call a poor human victory than you, but it is a victory. I could already have you with my body and soul. I'll wait for years if I must for you too to have a soul-body in order to love. We're still young, we can waste some time without wasting our whole lives. But look at everyone around you and see what we've made of ourselves and considered our daily victory. We haven't loved, that most of all. We haven't accepted what we don't understand because we don't want to look stupid. We've hoarded things and reassurances because we don't have each other. We don't have any joy that hasn't already been catalogued. We've built cathedrals, and stayed outside because the cathedrals we ourselves built, we're afraid they're traps. We haven't surrendered to ourselves, because that would be the start of a long life and we're afraid of that. We've avoided falling to our knees in front of the first one of us who says, out of love: you're afraid. We've organized smiley clubs and associations where you are served with or without soda. We've tried to save ourselves but without using the word salvation in order to avoid the embarrassment of being innocents. We haven't used the word love so as not to have to recognize its contexture of hate, love, jealousy and so many other contradictories. We've kept our death a secret in order to make our life possible. Many of us make art because we don't know what the other thing is like. We've disguised our indifference with false love, knowing that our indifference is disguised anguish. We've disguised with a small fear the greatest fear of all and that's why we never speak of what really matters. Speaking about what really matters is considered a blunder. We haven't worshipped because we have the sensible pettiness to remember on time the false gods. We haven't been pure and naive in order not to laugh at ourselves and so that at each day's close we can say "at least I didn't do something stupid" and that way we don't feel confused before putting out the light. We've smiled in public about things we wouldn't smile about alone. We've called our candor weakness. We have feared each other, most of all. And all this we consider our daily victory. But I escaped that, Lóri, I escaped with the ferocity of someone escaping the plague, Lóri, and I'll wait until you too are more ready.

Lóri was always amazed at how well Ulisses knew her. But despite his ability to understand, she feared his criticisms or that he might lose heart and abandon her, and had never told him that the "trouble" often returned: the air inside her would then smell of damp dust. Is it going to start up again, dear God? She'd then wonder. And gather all her strength to stop the pain. What pain was it? Of existing? Of belonging to some unknown thing? Of having been born?

And later, the pain staunched as if it had never been, exhausted, after having swum for miles in the empty universe, she'd throw herself panting on the shining sands of a planet, immobile, face down.

She also hadn't told Ulisses how the painful sensation of being unattached was less intense once she really was unattached: her father having lost most of his fortune, she'd moved on her own from Campos to Rio, bought the little apartment where she lived, provided for regally by an allowance from her father. With four brothers, and she the only daughter, her father sent her whatever she wanted. With a third of the fortune left over there was enough to live like the rich but luckily for her nonstop travel in Europe was no longer an option. She hadn't told Ulisses out of a sense of shame: he was, as far as she'd understood, a socialist and wouldn't without disgust or scorn let himself be friends with her without contempt.

—Why did you come to Rio? Aren't there primary schools in Campos?

—Because I didn't want ... didn't want to marry, I wanted a certain kind of freedom that wouldn't have been possible there without a scandal, in my family for starters, there everyone knows everything, my father sends me an allowance because with the money from the school I couldn't—

—How many lovers have you had? he interrupted.

She was silent. Then she said:

—They weren't quite lovers because I didn't love them.

—During the holidays, like now, don't you feel alone? Before me, I mean.

—I have some company because I can always chat a little with the maid I've had forever who spends hours tidying up the house and preparing lunch and dinner. And there's a fortune-teller I visit now and then.

He didn't laugh:

—And girlfriends, don't you miss not having them?

Since he hadn't laughed, she was able to say:

—But the fortune-teller is my friend, she doesn't even charge me. And I was tired of living with four brothers and my father and everyone we knew. I only had girlfriends when I was still in college. Now I prefer to be alone.

—Listen, Lóri, you know very well how I met you and I'd like to recall it for a reason: you were waiting for a taxi and I, after taking a long look at you, because I liked you physically, simply went up to you with some small talk about how hard it was to find a taxi at that time of the day, offered to drive you wherever you wanted, and after we'd been on the road for five minutes invited you to have a whiskey with me and you without any reluctance accepted. Did your lovers approach you in the street?

She was offended and replied harshly and sincerely:

—Of course not. I don't want to talk about them. They were of no importance, or just a relative and fleeting one. And I'm not even asking if you have a lover right now.

Neither said a word. He perhaps cautiously thinking that this was their first jealous scene. She happy, thinking it was their first jealous scene.

—How many lovers have you had? he asked abruptly.

She making an effort to control herself said quickly:

—Five.

He swallowed the pain and changed the subject:

—But on your travels it's impossible that you were never among orange trees, sun, and flowers with bees. Not just the dark cold but the rest too?

—No, she said gloomily. Those things are not for me. I'm a big-city woman.

—First of all, Campos isn't what you'd call a big city. And anyway those things, as symbols, are for everybody. You've just never learned to have them.

—And that can be learned? Orange trees, sun, and bees on flowers?

—It can when you no longer have your own nature as a powerful guide. Lóri, Lóri, listen: you can learn anything, even how to love! And the strangest thing, Lóri, is that you can learn to have joy!

—Tell me what you want me to learn, she said with unexpected irony. The Song of Songs?

—Maybe, why not? he'd replied more seriously.

—You say that because you're ready.

—I'll never be ready in every way, Lóri, I'm under no illusions about that.

They fell silent, Ulisses asked for another whiskey.

—Why, he asked, do you give me the impression that you've separated from other people voluntarily?

—One day I might tell you, if I pluck up the courage to talk a lot.

It was rare for him to show clearly that he was serious. Lóri recognized that he had concentration, intensity, delicacy and discretion, though all that was almost always wrapped in a light tone in order not to show his feelings.

—You know, Lóri, he said smiling now. After I'd met you three or four times—God, it might even have been the very first time I saw you!—I thought that I could treat you with the method of some artists: conceiving something and carrying it out at the same time. Because at first I thought I'd found a naked white canvas, and all I needed was to use my brushes. After that I discovered that if the canvas was naked it was also blackened by thick smoke, from some nasty fire, and that it wouldn't be easy to clean. No, to conceive and carry out is the great privilege of a few. But even so I didn't give up. No, he kept speaking as if she weren't there, with good intentions you really can't make literature: or life either. But there's something that isn't a good intention. It's a gentleness toward life that also demands the greatest courage to accept it.

Lóri didn't say anything. She realized that he was thinking aloud and that she didn't need to understand. But it was so good to listen. She also wanted to make herself heard and said with a certain voluptuousness in her voice, which didn't suit her and made him raise his eyebrows questioningly:

—I was reading a philosopher one day, you know. Once I followed a bit of his advice and it worked. It was more or less this: it's only when we forget all our knowledge that we begin to know. So I thought of you who speaks not a word of philosophy to me and when we're together, yes, when we're together you even seem like a wise man who no longer wants to be wise and who even, you know, even surrenders to the luxury of disguised worrying like any one of us.

Ulisses was watchful, motionless. Lóri went on:

—It seems so easy at first glance to follow someone's advice. Yours, for example.

Now she was speaking seriously:

—Your advice. But there's a great, the greatest obstacle for me to make progress: I myself. I've been the greatest hindrance along my path. It's with enormous effort that I manage to impose myself on myself.

She'd never spoken so many words at a stretch. That's why she wanted to avoid the main thing. Suddenly however she realized that if she didn't say the last thing, she wouldn't have said anything, and spoke:

—I'm an insurmountable mountain along my own path. But sometimes through a word of yours or a word I read, suddenly everything becomes clear.

Yes, everything sometimes would become clear and she'd emerge from herself almost with splendor.

—Yes, said Ulisses. But you're wrong. I don't give you advice. I just—I—I think that what I'm really doing is waiting. Waiting perhaps for you to give yourself advice, I don't know, Lóri, I swear I don't know, sometimes it seems like I'm wasting my time, sometimes it seems that on the contrary, there's no more perfect, though worrisome, way to use time: the time of waiting for you. Do you know how to pray?

—What? she asked with a start.

—Not pray the Lord's Prayer, but ask something of yourself, ask the maximum of yourself?

—I don't know if I know, I've never tried. Is that a piece of advice? she asked with irony.

He looked flustered:

—I think it was. Forget what I said.

BUT SHE DIDN'T FORGET.

She was washing her face slowly, combing her hair slowly, already in her nightdress. She was putting it off, putting it off. She brushed her teeth one more time. Her brow was wrinkled, her soul trembling. She knew she'd try to pray and was frightened. As if whatever she was going to ask of herself and of the God required great care: because whatever she asked, she would be given. She went to the fridge, drank a glass of water: acting as if she'd been hypnotized by Ulisses. And a tiny gesture of revolt against the hypnotism to which she'd apparently been subjected was making her delay whatever was coming.

Ask? How do you ask? And what do you ask for?

Do you ask for life?

You ask for life.

But don't you already have life?

There's a more real life.

What is real?

And she didn't know how to answer. Blindly she would have to ask. But she wanted, if she had to ask blindly, at least to understand what she was asking. She knew she shouldn't ask for the impossible: you can't ask for the answer. The big answer was not granted us. It is dangerous to meddle with the big answer. She preferred to ask humbly, not on her level, which was enormous: Lóri was feeling that she was an enormous human being. And that she should be careful. Or not? All her life she'd been careful not to be big inside herself so as not to be in pain.

No, she shouldn't ask for more life. For the time being that was dangerous. She knelt trembling beside the bed for that was how you prayed and said quietly, severely, sadly, mumbling her prayer with a bit of shame: relieve my soul, make me feel that Thy hand is holding mine, make me feel that death doesn't exist because in truth we are already in eternity, make me feel that loving is not dying, that the surrender of yourself doesn't mean death, make me feel a modest and daily joy, make me not ask Thee too much, because the answer would be as mysterious as the question, make me remember that there is also no explanation as to why a son wants his mother's kiss and yet he wants it and yet the kiss is perfect, make me receive the world without fear, since I was created for this incomprehensible world and I myself incomprehensible too, so there's a connection between this mystery of the world and our own, but that connection isn't clear to us as long as we hope to understand it, bless me so that I can experience with joy the bread I eat, the slumber I sleep, make me show kindness to myself because otherwise I won't be able to feel that God has loved me, make me lose the shame of wishing that at the hour of my death there will be a beloved human hand to hold mine, amen.

Not for nothing did she understand those who were seeking a path. How arduously she was seeking her own! And today how impatiently and roughly she was seeking her best way to be, her shortcut, since she no longer dared speak of a path. She was hanging on ferociously to her hunt for a way of walking, for the right steps. But the shortcut with refreshing shade and light flashing between the trees, the shortcut where she'd finally be herself, that she'd only felt in a certain indeterminate moment of the prayer. But she was also aware of something: when she was most ready, she'd move from herself to other people, her path was other people. When she could fully feel the other she'd be safe and think: here is my port of arrival.

But first she needed to reach herself, first she needed to reach the world.

WHEN THEY NEXT MET ON THE TERRACE OF THE BAR, a week later, Ulisses had his sluggish and uninterested look about him. But Lóri was familiar with it: he looked like this because he was calmly practicing instant by instant a way to clear a path. Whenever he returned from this distant gaze it was to look at her with a vague desire that didn't seem to want to grow stronger.

Lóri kept quiet, letting him drink in silence, without looking at him. So it gave her a little fright to she hear him address her, and she didn't know how long he'd been contemplating her before saying:

— You are so ancient, Lóri, he said and to her surprise there was tenderness in his voice. You're so ancient, my flower, that I should give you wine in an amphora, he said now without tenderness and he'd called her "my flower" the way she'd heard him call his secretary, that time they'd run into her on the street. It was a fake way of seeming like friends, just as Lóri was treating him with a certain dryness. But there was tenacity in Ulisses, there was tenacity in Lóri.

Ulisses was now looking at her with curiosity:

—Lóri, can't you at least feel what there is of profound and risky adventure in this thing we're attempting? Lóri, Lóri! We're attempting joy! Do you at least feel that? And feel how we're venturing into danger? Do you feel that there's more safety in dull pain? Ah Lóri, Lóri, can't you recover, at least hazily, in your flesh's memory, the pleasure that at least in the cradle you must have felt at being alive? At being? Or at least some other time in life, no matter when, nor why?

Lóri didn't reply, knowing that he could sense that the answer was negative.

—Do you prefer pain?

She didn't reply to that either, knowing he could sense that the answer would once again be: no.

—What is it? To learn joy, do you need every guarantee?

She remained silent, because Ulisses's tone had changed and instead of passionate had become sardonic and meant to wound her. He leaned back in his chair a bit tired and said:

—You're the type who needs guarantees. Do you want to know what I'm like in order to accept me? I'll let you get to know me better, he said with irony. Look, I've got a verbose soul and use few words. I'm irritable and easily hurt people. I'm also very calm and forgive immediately. I never forget. But there are few things I remember. I'm patient but quickly fly into a rage, like most patient people. People never really annoy me, no doubt because I forgive them in advance. I like people a lot for selfish reasons: it's because in the end they resemble me. I never forget an offense, that's true, but how can it be true, when offenses escape my mind as if they'd never come in?

Lóri was starting to think Ulisses was mocking her. And she pursed her lips in anger. Yet she couldn't help wanting to hear him out, her curiosity was increasing since, though she knew he was joking, he was also speaking the truth.

47

—I possess a deep peace, he continued, only because it is deep and cannot even be reached by myself. If I could grasp it, I wouldn't have a minute's peace. As for my superficial peace, it is an allusion to the true peace. Another thing I forgot is that there's another allusion inside me—to the wide and open world. I'm a professor of Philosophy because that's what I studied most and basically I like to hear myself talk about things that interest me. I have a feel for teaching that makes my students fall in love with the subject and look me up outside of class. This feel for teaching, which is a desire to impart knowledge, is something I have with you too, Lóri, even though you're my worst student. Anyway, though I look tough, which by the way partly comes from having such a straight nose, though I look tough, I'm full of so much love and that's no doubt what gives me a kind of grandeur, the grandeur you see and which scares you.

As if he'd suddenly realized that he'd been speaking seriously, he stopped and laughed in order to undo everything he'd said:

—My love for the world is like this: I forgive people for having a misshapen nose or lips that are too thin or for being ugly—every flaw or error in others is an opportunity for me to love. You see, I don't let anyone order me around, yet I don't mind for example simply following the teaching plan the university sets out for each class.

Ulisses finally saw Lóri's mute rage. So he said simply and sincerely:

—I know I was joking, but I didn't tell a single lie, everything I said was true. And if I confessed something, it doesn't matter, especially if it was to you. Though, by the way, I'd confess to others too, without any danger: nobody can make use of what other people are, not even mental use, that's why, this kind of confession is never dangerous. Maybe you know me even less now. The best way to throw someone off your scent is to tell the truth, though I've never tried to throw you off, Lóri, he said.

In some pain Lóri then realized that Ulisses, despite his claims to the contrary, didn't want to give himself to her. And she would respond with like for like. Maybe before he'd spoken, she'd intended to give herself to him one day, since she knew that she'd have to give what she was to someone, otherwise what would she do with herself? How to die before you give yourself, even in silence? Because by surrendering she'd finally have a witness to herself. And because Ulisses must also have thought of death, he said:

—Before dying you live, Lóri. It's a natural thing to die, to be transformed, to be transmuted. Nothing beyond dying has ever been invented. Just as no one's ever invented a different kind of bodily love which, nonetheless, is strange and blind and nonetheless each person, not knowing about anyone else, reinvents the copy. Dying must be a natural pleasure. After dying you don't go to paradise, dying is the paradise.

They sat in silence for a long time, a silence that wasn't heavy. Until he, as if wanting to give her something, said:

—Look at that sparrow, Lóri—he ordered—it keeps pecking the ground that looks empty but its eyes surely see food.

Obedient, she looked. And suddenly the sparrow took flight, and in her surprise Lóri forgot herself and like a child said to Ulisses:

—It's so pretty that it flies!

She'd spoken with the innocence she used in her lessons with the children, when she wasn't afraid of being judged. Anxiously she then glanced at Ulisses. He was looking at her. With a fright Lóri noticed: was it a look … of love?

A WEEK LATER LÓRI WAS STILL THINKING ABOUT THAT last meeting. She hadn't seen Ulisses since, nor had he called her. She'd been embroidering a tablecloth all week, and keeping her skillful hands busy she'd managed to pass the long days of the vacation. Embroidering, embroidering. Sometimes, when night fell, she'd take a long time making herself up and go to the movies.

But inside she was feeling an urgency, was in a hurry: there was something she needed to know and experience, and she didn't know what and never had. And somehow time was getting short, it wouldn't be long before the schools reopened. She was afraid Ulisses would get tired of her pachydermic resistance to letting the world enter her, and give up. And despair would overtake her. She knew she wasn't yet ready to surrender to him or anyone else, and in this interim he might leave her. During one of those sunny afternoons her despair grew. Suddenly she let herself lie face down on the bed, her face almost buried in her pillow: the pain had returned.

The pain had returned almost physically, and she thought

about praying. But she immediately discovered that she didn't want to speak to the God. Maybe never again. She remembered that once, on holiday on a farm, she'd lain face down in a clearing in a grove, resting her chest on the earth, her limbs on the earth, only her face turned toward the ground was protected in the crook of her arm.

Remembering that day, which she saw again, she thought that from now on this was all she wanted from the God: to rest her chest on him and not say a word. But if that were possible, it would only be after her death. As long as she was alive she'd have to pray, which she no longer wanted to do, or speak with the humans who would answer her and might represent God. Especially Ulisses.

Though Ulisses, through professional deformation, taught too much. Not that he had a professorial air, he looked more like an older student, whose words didn't come from books but from a life she suspected was full. Which didn't keep him from being unintentionally a bit pedantic. It annoyed her that he wanted to seem ... what? Superior? Ulisses, wise Ulisses, someday would fall like a statue from its pedestal. Lóri knew her thoughts were born of rage, of pain, with her face buried in her pillow.

She no longer knew anything. And despite now feeling mute before the God, she was aware in herself of an intense almost piercing desire to complain, to accuse, especially to claim what was hers. She felt she'd already experienced so much that now, according to the romantic logic of humans, the time had come for her to receive peace. She no longer dared think of joy, she didn't really know what that was, but of peace. What would joy be? Would she still be able to recognize it, if it came? Or was it already too late for her to know what it looked like. For she kept imagining that joy might come like a simple sound almost below what was audible. So she, who'd never again spoken to the cosmic God, said to Him in sudden rage: I'll give Thee nothing because Thou gavest me nothing.

Because she seemed to know that something existed—what—that humans gave the God—how? And she no longer even wanted to know what it was. Just that she felt that the God too needed humans—and so she refused herself to Him.

Could it be possible that at a certain point in life the world would become obvious? She was afraid of losing the life of continual surprise if she reached that point, and yet it would become a source of peace.

Wasn't peace what she wanted? Not that she could help herself, however, from almost enjoying what she imagined would happen after death—the way she'd rested her body on the earth, resting herself completely until she was absorbed by the God. She'd once wanted to be dead, not because she didn't want life—the life that still hadn't given her its secret—but because she longed for that integration without words. But the word of God was so completely mute that the silence was He Himself. She also no longer wanted to enter a church, not even just to inhale the cool and secluded half-light.

She was now alone for the pain that had to come. She knew that, if she was alone now and for the pain then it would come—but not from the humility of an acceptance or courage. But like a challenge to the God against whom now, out of disappointment and solitude, she seemed to want to test her strength. Thou hast created me through a father and a mother and then abandoned me in the desert. In some strange vengeance, since it was against herself, against a child of the God, she would then stay in the desert, and without asking for water to drink. The one who'd suffer most from this was her, but the main thing is that with her voluntary suffering she was offending the God and so she hardly minded the pain.

But her God was of no use to her: He had been made in her own image, looked too much like her, fretted about solutions—except in Him it was creative anxiety—the same severity she had. And when He was good, He was just the way she would be if she had goodness. The true God, not made in her image and likeness, was therefore completely misunderstood by her, and she didn't know if He could understand her. Her God had been terrestrial until now, and no longer was. From now on, if she wanted to pray, it would be like praying blindly to the cosmos and to the Nothing. And above all she could no longer ask the God for anything. She discovered that until now she had prayed to an I-myself, but one that was powerful, magnified and omnipotent, calling it the God and the way a child sees in his father the figure of a king.

Then Lóri woke a little to a more objective reality around her, changed the position of her head on her bent arm. She reflected that she'd been struggling with the God for some minutes, tired, exhausted, she murmured without any modulation in her voice: I don't understand anything. It was such an indubitable truth that both her body and her soul sagged somewhat and so she rested a little. In that instant she was just one of the women of the world, and not an I, and joined as if for an eternal and aimless march of men and women on pilgrimage toward the Nothing. What was a Nothing was exactly the Everything.

She had demystified one of the few glories from which she lived.

She knew that for now she was hurting a lot and that later

she'd hurt even more because she'd suffer the lack of That which, even if it didn't exist, she loved because she was one of its cells. And she might be saved: because anguish was the inability to feel pain at last. She thought: I never had my own pain. Through a lack of glory, she'd suffered manageably whatever she had to suffer inside her. But now on her own, loving a God that no longer existed, she might finally touch the pain that was her own. Anguish too was the fear of finally feeling pain.

She was already missing what had been: she wouldn't even visit Santa Luzia church, which was her refuge from the numbing heat of the city, anymore. She was remembering the last time she'd gone in and sat in the limpid shade amid the saints. She'd thought: "Christ was Christ for others, but who? Who was a Christ for Christ?" He'd had to go directly to the God. And she, as she sat in the pew, had also wanted to be able to go directly to the Omnipotence, without having to go through Christ's human condition which was also hers and everyone else's. And, oh God, not wanting to go to Him through the merciful condition of Christ might once again be nothing more than the fear of loving. She got up and went back to her embroidery.

That's when the phone rang. Even before answering she knew it had to be Ulisses. She put her embroidery on a chair and let the phone ring a little more, not wanting to look too eager.

Yes, it was him. And as if a week hadn't gone by, he said he was at his club's pool and why didn't she meet him there, all she had to say at the gate was that she was his guest. She didn't want to see him at the pool, but the fear of losing him made her agree, though fearing the moment they'd see each other almost naked.

An hour and a half later—the time needed to buy a new swimsuit—she was changed in a cubicle, and without the courage to go out. She wrapped herself in the bathrobe and went out to find him sitting on the edge of the pool. She tried to hide her deep reluctance to appear practically naked, finally took off the robe, she wasn't even looking at him. They sat without speaking, he was drinking a gin and tonic.

A lot of time had passed or maybe not much but for her the silence was becoming intolerable, while to hide it she was swinging her feet in the green water. Until at last he spoke and without crudeness said:

—Look at that girl over there, for example, the one in the red swimsuit. Look how she walks with the natural pride of someone who has a body. You, besides hiding what is called the soul, are ashamed to have a body.

She didn't reply, but, struck, became imperceptibly stiffer. Afterward, sensing he wasn't going to say anything else, she slowly managed to relax her muscles. She thought—inasmuch as she could think while wearing a swimsuit in front of him— she thought: how could I explain to him, even if I wanted to, and she didn't want to, the long journey she'd taken to reach that possible moment in which her legs were swinging in the pool. And he didn't think it was a big deal. How to explain that, coming from as far away inside herself as she had, being half-alive was already a victory. Because finally, once the fright of being naked in front of him was broken, she was breathing calmly, already half-alive.

As she made a movement, which was to toss her hair back, she glimpsed his face, and realized he was looking at her and desiring her. She then felt an embarrassment that was now different from what he'd called her embarrassment about having a body. It was the embarrassment of someone who desires too, as Lóri had desired to press her chest and limbs against the God. Feeling very clearly her own desire, she became skittish and hard, and they sat in silence for the rest of the afternoon. She gradually calmed down and lost her greatest fear: that she'd lose him because she was taking so long.

Her own thought surprised: so she really was planning to be his one day? Since she was always fooling herself into thinking it was an odd kind of friendship and would stay that way forever, until withering like a fruit that isn't harvested in time and falls rotten from the tree to the ground.

The children's cries of joy and fright could no longer be heard: it was much later and the sun was weaker, the pool empty. How long had they spent in silence? Their solitude was only interrupted by the silent and eager arrival of the waiter who would come fill Ulisses's glass as soon as it was emptied.

The silence of the dusk. She looked at Ulisses, and he was looking into the distance with half-closed eyes. She looked at him. And at that hour a luminosity was coming off him. Then Lóri realized that the brilliance was the sun's flashing before definitively dying. She looked at the little tables with parasols arranged around the pool: they seemed to hover in the homogeneity of the cosmos. Everything was infinite, nothing had a beginning or an end: that was the cosmic eternity. Then in an instant the vision of reality was coming undone, it had only been a split second, the homogeneity was disappearing and her gaze was getting lost in a multiplicity of still-surprising tonalities: after the sharp and instantaneous vision something had followed that was more recognizable on earth. As for Ulisses, in these new colors that Lóri could finally see, as for Ulisses he was now both solid and transparent, which enriched him with resonances and splendor. You could say he was a handsome man.

For the first time then she looked at him from the perspective of strictly masculine beauty, and saw there was in him a calm virility. In the new light, Ulisses was unreal and yet plausible. Unreal because of his kind of beauty, which was now flickering with the last flickers of the sun. Plausible because all you'd have to do was reach out your hand and, in whatever it touched, you'd find the resistance of all solid things. Lóri was afraid of what could happen to her, since she was a worshipper of men.

Ulisses turned his face toward her and discovered he was being inspected. However, being caught, it was Lóri who blushed, averting her eyes.

—Don't be afraid, he said smiling, don't be afraid of my silence … I'm a madman but I'm guided by some great sage inside me …

So he hadn't understood her: he'd thought she was bothered by the silence. Lóri didn't reply. She was already used to Ulisses's didactic tone which actually wasn't pedantic. She glanced at him: he was so calm as if she were the only one suffering and he'd never known the pain of having no future except that of continuing to exist. He hadn't understood her, and that made her happy. So Lóri discovered what was happening with great delicacy: what she'd thought was just her direct gaze at Ulisses and his reality had been the first frightening step toward something. Or had he noticed? He'd noticed, she felt, but without knowing what it was all about, he'd felt that she'd moved ahead and so he'd wanted to reassure her with the assurance of resuming his silence.

For it was as if she were in her early childhood and unafraid that the anguish might arise: she was in enchantment by the oriental colors of the Sun which was tracing gothic figures in the shadows. Since the God was born of Nature and He in turn meddled with it. The last lights were undulating on the standing green water of the pool. Discovering the sublime in the trivial, the invisible underneath the tangible—she herself completely disarmed as if in that instant she'd learned that her ability to uncover the secrets of natural life was still intact. And also disarmed by the slight anguish that came to her when she felt she could uncover other secrets too, perhaps a mortal secret. But she knew she was ambitious: she'd scorn easy success and want, though she was afraid, to rise higher and higher or descend lower and lower.

Ulisses spoke:

—Nice and easy, Lóri, take it nice and easy. But be careful. It's better not to speak, not to tell me. There's a great silence inside me. And this silence has been the source of my words. And from the silence has come the most precious thing of all: silence itself.

—Why do you look at each person so carefully?

She blushed:

—I didn't know you were observing me. It's not for nothing that I look: it's because I like to see people being.

So saying she surprised herself and that seemed to bring her to vertigo. Because she, by surprising herself, was being. Even taking the chance that Ulisses wouldn't notice, she said very quietly to him:

—I am being …

—What? he asked when hearing that whispered voice of Lóri's.

— Nothing, it doesn't matter.

—Of course it does. Would you mind saying it again?

She grew more humble, because she'd already lost the strange and enchanted moment in which she'd been being:

—I said to you —Ulisses, I am being.

He looked closely at her and for a moment it was strange,

that familiar woman's face. He found himself strange, and understood Lóri: he was being.

They didn't say a word as if they'd just met for the first time. They were being.

—Me too, Ulisses said quietly.

Both knew that a great step had been taken in the apprenticeship. And there was no danger of wasting this feeling out of fear of losing it, because being was infinite, infinite like the waves of the sea. I am being, the tree in the garden was saying. I am being, said the approaching waiter. I am being, said the green water in the pool. I am being, said the blue sea of the Mediterranean. I am being, said our green and treacherous sea. I am being, said the spider and stunned its prey with its venom. I am being, said a child who'd slipped on the tiles and cried out in fear: Mama! I am being, said the mother who had a son who was slipping on the tiles around the pool. But the light was going quiet for the night and they were surprised again, the dusky light. Lóri was fascinated by this meeting with herself, she fascinated herself and almost hypnotized herself.

There they were. Until the light that preceded the dusk started thinning out between shadows and greater transparencies, and the sky threatened a revelation. The light was turning spectral into near absence, though that kind of neutrality wasn't yet touched by the darkness: it didn't look like dusk but instead like the most imponderable part of a dawn. All that was absolutely impossible, that's why Lóri knew she was seeing it. If it were something reasonable, she would have known nothing of it.

And when everything started to get unbelievable, night fell.

Lóri, for the first time in her life, felt a power that was starting to seem like a threat to what she'd been until then. She then spoke her soul to Ulisses:

—One day it will be the world with its haughty impersonality versus my extreme individuality as a person but we'll be one and the same.

She looked at Ulisses with the humility she was suddenly feeling and saw with surprise his surprise. Only then was she surprised at herself. The two looked at each other in silence. She seemed to be asking for help against what she'd somehow involuntarily said. And he with moist eyes didn't want her to flee and said:

—Say that again, Lóri.

—I no longer know what it was.

—But I do, I'll always know. You literally said: one day it will be the world with its haughty impersonality versus my extreme individuality as a person but we'll be one and the same.

—Yes.

Lóri was softly astounded. So this was happiness. At first she felt empty. Then her eyes moistened: it was happiness, but how mortal I am, how the love for the world transcends me. Love for mortal life was killing her sweetly, bit by bit. And what can I do? What can I do with happiness? What can I do with this strange and piercing peace, which is already starting to hurt me like an anguish, like a great silence of spaces? To whom can I give my happiness, which is already starting to scratch me a bit and scares me. No, I don't want to be happy. I prefer mediocrity. Ah, thousands of people don't have the nerve to linger a while longer in this unknown thing which is feeling happy and they prefer mediocrity. She said goodbye to Ulisses almost in a run: he was the danger.

THAT NIGHT LÓRI STAYED AWAKE.

It was a very lovely night: it looked like the world. Dark space was studded with stars, the sky in mute eternal watchfulness. And the earth below with its mountains and its seas.

Lóri was sad. It wasn't a difficult sadness. It was more like a sadness of longing. She was alone. With eternity in front of and behind her. The human is alone.

She wanted to step back. But she kept feeling it was too late: once the first step was taken it was irreversible, and kept pushing her on to more, more, more! What do I want, my God. The thing is she wanted everything.

As if she were passing from the man-ape to pithecanthropus erectus. And then there was no going back: the struggle for survival among mysteries. And the thing the human being aspires to most is to become a human being.

Since she wasn't sleepy, she went to the kitchen to warm up some coffee. She put too much sugar in the cup and the coffee was dreadful. This brought her to a more everyday reality. She rested a bit from being.

She was hearing the sound of the waves of the sea of Ipanema breaking on the beach. It was a different night, because while Lóri was thinking and doubting, everyone else was sleeping. She went to the window, looked at the street with its few streetlamps and the stronger smell of the sea. It was dark for Lóri. So dark. She thought about people she knew: they were sleeping or having fun. Some were drinking whiskey. Her coffee then became even sweeter, even more impossible. And the darkness of loners grew so much greater.

She was falling into a sadness without pain. It wasn't bad. It was part of life, certainly. The next day she would probably have some joy, also without great ecstasies, just a little joy, and that wasn't bad either.

That's how she tried to make peace with the mediocrity of living.

But it was late: she was already yearning for new ecstasies of joy or of pain. What she needed was everything the most human of humans had. Even if it was pain, she'd bear it, unafraid of again wanting to die. She'd bear everything. Provided she was given everything.

No. No one would give it to her. She herself would have to be the one to try to get it. Ill at ease, she kept pacing her apartment, without anywhere she wanted to sit. Her guardian angel had abandoned her. She herself had to be her own guardian.

And she now had a responsibility to be herself. In this world of choices, she seemed to have chosen.

Once again she went to the window: she saw the landscape that was familiar to her by day but strange by night. That high dark and shifting and trembling shadow was the tree that by day would flash sun among its leaves. Now they were quivering in the wind that kept pulling scraps of paper along the curb, making them almost fly. It was windy, and Lóri was afraid that it would rain in the morning and she couldn't do what she was planning: go to the beach. Though she knew that even if it did rain she would go. She was from Campos, land without sea, and had never managed to get into the habit of going to the beach that was so close to her apartment.

Without noticing, she fell asleep sitting in one of the arm-chairs. And immediately dreamed that Ulisses that very night was with some other woman. The jealousy woke her with a start. Was she going to suffer that too? Yes, jealousy too, rage too, everything too.

It was still night, she must have just slept for a few minutes. But she didn't feel tired: she was alert.

So was there some thing you could learn ... what? She'd gradually find out, no doubt. Lóri wanted to learn, she didn't know where to start and was also ashamed. The way they had been at the pool and there not only had she figured out the fairylike and at the same time opaque transformation of the sun for the first time, the way she'd felt the world, she was now going to experience the world on her own in order to see what it was like. But this time not at the pool, where she'd find people, but in the sea, at an hour when no one would turn up.

She fell back asleep and this time more deeply for when with a kind of start she awoke it was already light. She looked at the clock: it was ten past five on a clear and limpid morning. The beach would still be deserted and what was she going to learn? She'd go out as if toward the nothing.

She put on her bathing suit and robe, and without breaking her fast walked to the beach. It was so lovely and fresh on the street! Where no one was about, except the milkman's cart in the distance. She kept walking and looking, looking, looking, seeing. This time it was a bodily wrestling with herself. Dark, wounded, and blind—how to find in this wrestling a diamond that was tiny but fairylike, as fairylike as she imagined pleasures should be. Even if she didn't find them now, she was aware, her need would not flag. Would she win or lose? But she'd continue her wrestling with life. Not even with her own life, but with life. Something had unlocked within her, at last.

And there it was, the sea.

THERE WAS THE SEA, THE MOST UNINTELLIGIBLE OF nonhuman existences. And there was the woman, standing, the most unintelligible of living beings. Since the human being had one day asked a question about itself, it had become the most unintelligible of the beings in whom blood circulates. She and the sea.

There could only be a meeting of their mysteries if one surrendered to the other: the surrender of two unknowable worlds done with the trust with which two understandings might surrender to each other.

Lóri was gazing at the sea, that was what she could do. It was only marked off for her by the line of the horizon, that is, by her human incapacity to see the curve of the earth.

It must be six in the morning. The free dog was hesitating on the beach, the black dog. Why is a dog so free? Because he's the living mystery that doesn't ask itself questions. The woman hesitates because she's about to go in.

Her body takes comfort in its own smallness in relation to the vastness of the sea because it is the body's smallness that lets it become hot and marked-off, and that was making her a poor and free person, with her share of the freedom a dog has in the sands. That body will enter the unlimited cold that roars without rage in the silence of the dawn.

The woman doesn't realize: but she's carrying out an act of courage. With the beach empty at this hour, she can't copy other humans who make going into the sea one of life's simple lighthearted games. Lóri is alone. The salty sea is not alone because it's salty and big, and that's an achievement of Nature. Lóri's courage is that, not knowing herself, she still presses on, and acting without knowing yourself demands courage.

She enters. The very salty water is so cold that it gives her gooseflesh and mounts a ritual of attack on her legs.

But a fated joy—joy is a matter of fate—already took hold of her, though it doesn't occur to her to smile. To the contrary, she's very serious. There's a dizzying sea smell that stirs her from the sleep of ages.

And now she's alert, even without thinking, as a fisherman is alert without thinking. The woman is now a compact and a light and a sharp one—and heads through the iciness that, liquid, resists her, and yet lets her enter, as in love where resistance can be a secret request.

Walking slowly her secret courage grows—and suddenly she lets herself be covered by the first wave! The salt, the iodine, all the liquid leave her for a moment blind, dripping—standing shocked, fertilized.

Now that her entire body is drenched and water is pouring from her hair, now the cold becomes frigid. Advancing, she opens the waters of the world down the middle. She no longer needs courage, now she's an old hand at the ritual abandoned millennia ago. She lowers her head into the sparkle of the sea, and pulls out a head of hair that pours down over salty eyes that burn. She plays with her hand in the water, taking her time, her hair in the sun almost immediately stiffening with salt. With the conch of her hands and the haughtiness of people who never will offer explanations even to themselves: with the conch of her hands full of water, she drinks it in great gulps, good for a body's health.

And that's what she's been missing: the sea inside like the thick liquid of a man.

Now she's entirely like herself. Her nourished throat tightens with salt, her eyes go red from the drying salt, the waves crash against her and retreat, crash and retreat since she's a compact barrier.

She dives once again, once again she drinks more water, now no longer greedy since she already knows and already has a rhythm of life in the sea. She's the lover who is fearless because she knows she'll have it all again.

The sun comes out more and makes her shiver as it dries her, she dives again: each time less greedy and less sharp. Now she knows what she wants: she wants to stand still in the sea. So she does. As if against the sides of a ship, the water crashes, retreats, crashes, retreats. The woman isn't receiving transmissions or sending them. She doesn't need communication.

Then she walks inside the water back to the beach, and the waves push her gently helping her come out. She's not walking on the waters—ah she'd never do that since walking on the waters had already been done millennia ago—but no one can take this away from her: walking inside the waters. Sometimes the sea resists her exit by pushing her forcefully back, but then the woman's prow advances a bit harder and rougher.

And now she steps onto the sand. She knows she's shining

with water, and salt and sun. Even if she forgets, she'll never be able to lose all this. In some obscure way her streaming hair is something from a shipwreck. Because she knows—knows she's done a danger. A danger as ancient as human beings.

LÓRI HAD GONE FROM THE RELIGION OF HER CHILD-hood to a nonreligion and now had gone to something more ample: she'd reached the point of believing in a God so vast that he was the world with its galaxies: that was what she'd seen the day before when she entered the deserted sea on her own. And because of his impersonal vastness this was a God you couldn't implore: what you could do was join him and be big too.

To compensate, because when in pain she couldn't stop imploring, she'd learned from one day to the next to implore herself for mercy and strength, since she wasn't so vast or impersonal or unreachable. And she'd received enough mercy at least to get her breath back.

Her pain in life had now taken the form of being unable to wait without anguish for Ulisses to call. She herself had only called him a few times.

This time she was even more eager to meet him, she wanted him to know somehow about her dawn dip in the sea. But the phone was silent. And Lóri was afraid that, for lack of communication, she'd forfeit her steps forward.

It was the day the Organization of Primary Schools was throwing their back-to-school cocktail party, at the Museum of Modern Art. She wouldn't go, she'd wait for a possible call from Ulisses. But the hours passed, and she had a hunch that he wouldn't call. She remembered that at one cocktail party she'd met a man who became her lover for several months. And she thought maybe she should go to the party to "get herself" another man in order to free herself from the idea of Ulisses.

She felt life once again slipping through her fingers. In her humility she forgot that she herself was a source of life and of creation. So she'd rarely go out, didn't accept invitations. She wasn't a woman who always noticed a man's interest in her unless he told her—then she'd be astonished and accept.

First she called her fortune-telling friend who emboldened her. How could she, a grown woman, be so meek? How did she not realize that lots of men wanted her? How not to realize that she should, within the bounds of her dignity, have a love affair?

—At Maria's party, the fortune-teller said, I saw you enter the room where you knew everyone. And no one there was, as it happened, remotely equal to you, in educational skills, in intuitive understanding, and even in feminine charm. And yet you entered the room as timidly as if you weren't there, like a doe with its head down.

—But that's because ..., Lóri tried to defend herself, because I feel I'm so ... so nothing.

—That's not what the cards say. You need to walk with your head held high, you have to suffer because you're different from other people—cosmically different, that's what your cards say, so accept that you can't have the middle-class life other people do and go to the party today, and walk into the room with your head held high.

—But I haven't gone out for so long that I've forgotten how. And walk into a room full of people all by myself? Wouldn't it be better if I arranged to go with a girlfriend?

—No. You don't need company in order to go, you yourself are enough.

What her friend had told her, she thought as she hung up the phone, went well with the new attitude she'd been wanting to have since she'd gone into the sea, no, no, since she'd been at the pool with Ulisses. So, courageously she didn't arrange to go to the party with any other teacher, male or female—she'd risk it by herself.

She put on a fairly new dress, wanting to be ready to meet some man, but courage didn't come. So, without understanding what she was doing—she only understood afterward—she put too much makeup on her eyes and mouth until her powder-white face looked like a mask: she was putting someone else on top of herself: that someone was fantastically uninhibited, was vain, was proud of herself. That someone was exactly what she wasn't.

When it was time to go, she lost her nerve: wasn't she asking too much of herself? Wasn't going alone just showing off? All ready, with a painted mask on her face—ah "persona," how not to use you and be!—discouraged, she sat in the armchair in the living room she knew so well and her heart was asking her not to go. It was as if it foresaw that she was going to get hurt a lot and she wasn't a masochist. Finally she stubbed out her cigarette-for-courage, got up and went.

It seemed to her that a shy person's tortures had never been completely described—in the taxi that sped along she was dying a bit.

And suddenly there she was in front of an uncommonly large room with lots of people, perhaps, though it didn't look like many in the enormous space where like a ritual the cocktail party was unfolding.

How long did she bear it with her head held falsely high? The mask was making her uncomfortable, she knew moreover that she was prettier without makeup. But without makeup it would be the nakedness of soul. And she still couldn't risk that or allow herself that luxury.

Smiling she talked to one man, smiling she talked to another. But as at all cocktail parties, at this one too conversation was impossible and, when she noticed, she was alone again. She saw two men who had been her lovers, they exchanged vain words. And she saw with pain that she no longer desired them. She'd rather suffer from love than feel indifferent. But she wasn't indifferent: she was quite moved, she hadn't seen people for so long. She didn't know what to do: she wanted to leave like someone who was sobbing. But she kept up her pose and stayed a bit longer.

Until she felt that she could no longer bear to hold her head up, despite the two whiskeys she'd had. But how could she cross the enormous expanse to the door? Alone, like a runaway? She saw she'd reached the impasse of herself. So, with mumbled words, she confessed her drama to one of the other teachers, telling her she didn't want to leave alone and the girl, understanding her, brought her to the door.

And in the darkness of that night which already had a touch of autumn Lóri was an unhappy woman. Yes, she was different. But yes, she was shy. Yes, she was hypersensitive. Yes, she'd seen two men who had been her lovers and now were just semi-friends. The darkness of the autumn night in which the wind blew freshly rocking with delicacy the heavy branches of the trees. The perfume of the night. She had always known how to sense the smell of nature. With some pleasure—the only pleasure of the party—she crossed the ... Overpass (what was it called?). She finally found a cab in which she sat almost crying tears of relief, remembering that the same thing had happened to her in Paris but worse, since now she was more rooted in the earth.

The way the taxi driver looked at her led her to guess: she was so made-up that he'd probably taken her for a prostitute. "Persona." Lóri's memory wasn't great, that's why she didn't know if it was in the ancient Greek or Roman theatre that the actors, before going on stage, would stick on a mask whose expression represented the role they were to express. Lóri was well aware that one of the qualities of an actor was in sensitive changes of facial expression, and that the mask would hide those changes. So why did she like the idea of actors going on stage without their own faces so much? Maybe she thought that the mask was a giving of oneself as important as giving oneself through the pain of the face. Teenagers too, who were all face, as they were living their lives were making their own masks. And with much pain. Because knowing that from then on you'll be playing a role was a frightening surprise. It was the horrible freedom of not-being. And the moment of decision.

Lóri too was wearing the clown's mask of excessive makeup. The same one that in the birth pains of adolescence you'd choose so as not to be naked for the rest of the struggle. No, it's not that it would have been wrong to leave your own face exposed to feeling. But because if that face were naked it could, when injured, close into a sudden mask, involuntary and terrible: so it was less dangerous to choose, before that inevitably happened, to choose on your own to be a "persona." Choosing your own mask was the first voluntary human act. And solitary. But when you finally buckled on the mask of whatever you'd chosen to play yourself and play the world, your body would gain a new firmness, your head could sometimes hold itself high like the head of someone who has overcome an obstacle: the person was.

Though something humiliating could still happen. As it was now in the taxi with Lóri. Because, after years of relative success with the mask, suddenly—ah less than suddenly, because of a glance or an overheard word from the driver—suddenly her life's war mask was being singed like dry mud, and its jagged pieces were falling to the floor with a hollow clap. And there was her face naked now, mature, sensitive when it was no longer meant to be. And the face with its singed mask was crying in silence in order not to die.

She entered her house like a fugitive from the world. There was no point in hiding it: the truth was she didn't know how to live. It was nice to be home, she looked at herself in the mirror while washing her hands and saw the "persona" buckled to her face. She looked like a dolled-up monkey. Her eyes, under the thick makeup, were tiny and neutral, as if Intelligence had not yet revealed itself in mankind. So she washed her face, and was relieved to have a naked soul again. Then she took a pill to help her sleep and forget how her bravado had failed. Before sleep came, she was alert and promised herself never again to take a risk without protection.

The sleeping pill had started to calm her down. And the unfathomable night of dreams began, vast, levitating.

WHEN TWO WEEKS LATER ULISSES FINALLY CALLED—
he never chatted on the phone, just tersely said when and
where they'd meet and without asking if she wanted to go—
when he finally called to make a date, with the unexpected relief from pain, after hanging up she started crying briefly, more
a spasm of happiness than crying.

Then she calmed down and got dressed. She'd take advantage of the day's unseasonal heat, which would only ruin
makeup, to go without any. Without a mask. She was feeling
safer for having gone into the sea on her own and was going to
see if she'd dare tell Ulisses about her victory.

It was this time, walking over to the bar and before he saw
her, this time after days of pain unlocking, that when she saw
him seated with a glass of whiskey—unexpectedly the vision
of the two of them, still in the distance, unleashed in her a
happy and terrible human greatness, his greatness and hers.
She stopped for an instant, stunned. She looked afraid to
be advancing inside herself maybe too fast and with all the
risks—toward what?

In that instant he spotted her and with his unaffected gallantry rose to greet her. That meant Lóri had to approach while he gazed at her, which was still hard because she hadn't fully recovered either from going into the sea or from the sight of Ulisses beside the pool, she mixed both sensations into a single shy victory.

And as she was moving toward him, slowly, hesitantly as always, she saw that what she'd seen in Ulisses and had lit her up with its brightness in the middle of the pool was still there, though now mild enough to let her think that Ulisses—though he couldn't be called levelheaded because of the liberty that in him took the appearance of daring originality—Ulisses was a spartan man, free even of the sin of being a romantic.

When she finally reached his table—they never shook hands—Lóri had already though barely consciously started to feel proud of Ulisses as if he were hers, and this was new. In a way he was, because as soon as Lóri could transform herself he'd be hers, she imagined despite her doubts. What she was afraid of was one of Ulisses's qualities: his frankness. She was afraid that, if she advanced to the point of being readier and came to accept drawing close to him, he with his frankness might simply tell her it was too late. Because even fruits have seasons.

They sat down. And her earlier shyness had overtaken her at the thought of telling him about that serious moment of entering the sea. Since it had been more of a ritual than … than what?

—I, she said but then fell silent: she was too moved to speak.

—Yes? Ulisses encouraged her, leaning forward because he'd sensed that she had something important to say.

Then, as if throwing herself without a second thought into an abyss, Lóri said:

—One day at dawn I went to the sea on my own, there was nobody on the beach, I went into the water, there was just one black dog but far away from me!

He looked at her carefully, at first as if he hadn't understood what uncommon meaning there could be in that emotional declaration. At last as if he'd understood, he asked slowly:

—Did you enjoy it?

—I did, she replied humbly, and out of shame her eyes filled with tears that wouldn't fall, they just made her eyes look like two full pools. No, she then corrected herself, looking for the exact term, it's not that I enjoyed it. It's something else.

—Better or worse than enjoying?

—It was so different that I can't compare them.

He looked at her closely for a moment:

—I know, he then said.

And added simply:

—I love you.

She looked at him with darkened eyes but her lips trembled. They sat silently for a moment.

—Your eyes, he said changing his tone entirely, are bewildered but your mouth has that inner passion you fear. Your face, Lóri, is a mystery like the sphinx's: decipher me or I'll devour you.

She was surprised that he too had noticed what she'd seen of herself in the mirror.

—My mystery is simple: I don't know how to be alive.

—Because you only know, or only knew, how to be alive through pain.

—That's right.

—And don't you know how to be alive through pleasure?

—I almost do. That's what I was trying to tell you.

There was a long pause between them. Now Ulisses was the one who seemed moved. He called the waiter over, asked for another whiskey. After the waiter left, he said in a tone of voice as if he'd changed the subject and yet the subject was the same:

—Well, I had to pay my debt of joy to a world that was so often hostile to me.

—Living, she said in that incongruous dialogue in which they seemed to understand each other, living is so out of the ordinary that I'm only alive because I was born. I know that anyone could say the same, but the fact is I'm the one saying it.

—You still haven't got used to living? Ulisses asked with intense curiosity.

—No.

—Then that's perfect. You're the right woman for me. Because in my apprenticeship I'm missing someone to say obvious things in such an extraordinary way. Obvious things, Lóri, are the hardest truths to see—and to keep the conversation from getting too serious he added with a smile—Sherlock Holmes was aware of that.

—But it's sad to only see obvious things the way I do and find them strange. It's so strange. Suddenly it's as if I opened my closed hand and found a stone: a rough diamond in its raw form. Oh God, I don't even know what I'm talking about anymore.

They sat in silence.

—I've never spoken this much, Lóri said.

—With me you'll speak your whole soul, even in silence. One day I'll speak my whole soul, and we won't run dry because the soul is infinite. And besides we have two bodies which will be a joyful, mute, deep pleasure for us.

Lóri, to Ulisses's delighted surprise, blushed.

He looked closely at her and said:

—Lóri, you've gone red yet you've had five lovers.

She bowed her head, not in guilt but as a child hides its face. That's what Ulisses thought and his heart beat joyfully. Because he was infinitely further along in the apprenticeship: he could recognize in himself the joy and the victory.

Again they lapsed into silence. As if feeling they'd said more than she could, at present, bear, Ulisses struck a lighter and more casual tone:

—How long since you completed your training, I mean, to be a teacher?

—Five years.

—Are you all about the number five? he asked smiling. I bet you were top of your year.

She was surprised:

—How did you know?

—Because your fellow students must have been busy with life, and you, in order not to suffer, must have devoted yourself body and soul to your studies. I bet you're also one of the best teachers at your school.

—For the same reason? she asked sadly.

—Yes. I don't mean there's always only one reason for being among the best. I, for example, am supposed to be one of the best professors in my university. Firstly because the subject always excited me and I expected it to answer my questions, to make me think. I take enormous pleasure in thinking, Lóri. Later, I was lucky to have great teachers, as well as simultaneously being an autodidact: I spent almost all my money back then buying ridiculously expensive books. Another bit of luck for me as a teacher: my students love me. But I was also living, and I keep living now. Whereas you're a good teacher but you might not even let yourself laugh with your pupils. Later you'll learn, Lóri, and then you'll experience in full the great joy of communicating, of imparting.

Lóri sat there silent and serious.

—Lóri, read this poem and understand—he pulled a crumpled piece of paper from his pocket—I write poetry not because I'm a poet but to exercise my soul, it's man's most profound exercise. In general what comes out is incongruous, and it rarely has a theme: it's more like research into how to think. This one might have come out with a meaning that's easier to grasp.

She read the poem, didn't understand anything and gave him back the sheet, in silence.

—If I ever write an essay again, I'll want it to be the greatest. And the greatest should be said with the mathematical perfection of music, transposed to the deep rapture of a feeling-thought. Not quite transposed, since the process is the same, except music and words use different tools. There must, there has to, be a way to reach that. My poems are unpoetic but my essays are long poems in prose, in which I exercise to the maximum my ability to think and intuit. We, people who write, have in the human word, written or spoken, a great mystery that I don't want to unmask with my reasoning which is cold. I must not question the mystery in order not to betray the miracle. Whoever writes or paints or teaches or dances or does mathematical calculations, is working miracles every day. It's a great adventure and demands much courage and devotion and much humility. Humility in living isn't my strong point. But when I write I'm fated to be humble. Though within limits. Because the day I lose my own importance inside me—all will be lost. Conceitedness would be better, and the person who thinks he's the center of the world is closer to salvation, which is a silly thought, of course. What you can't do is stop loving yourself with a certain immodesty. To keep my strength, which is as great and helpless as that of any man who has respect for human strength, in order to keep it I have no modesty, unlike you.

They sat in silence.

—Instead of a guarana soda, can I have a whiskey? she asked.

—Of course, he said as he waved the waiter over. Are you trying to intensify this moment with the whiskey?

—Yes, she replied, surprised by his explanation.

She didn't know how to drink: she drank quickly as if it were soda. Soon, a little bashfully, she asked for another.

Ulisses smiled, as he called for the waiter.

—Drink more slowly or it'll go straight to your head. And also because drinking isn't about getting drunk, it's something else. Perhaps because I'm an old relic, I like seeing a woman who doesn't drink.

The waiter came over, served her, adding more ice.

—And your ancestors, Lóri?

—I don't know what you mean, but if it's about my family, only my father's left, and four brothers. I don't get along with them. They tried to make an impression on me but they were never that important in my life, and even less so once they lost most of their money and almost the majority of the servants. I took advantage of the chaos to come to Rio. It was an odd and nice experience to go from the big rooms of the family home, in Campos, to the tiny apartment that would have fitted in its entirety into one of the house's smaller rooms. I felt I'd returned to my true proportions. And the freedom, of course.

—And who was important in your life?

—Nobody.

—Did people fall in love with you?

—Yes.

—I thought so. I, for reasons unknown, ever since I was a lad had a talent: of awakening something in women. Doesn't your gift for attracting men affect you?

She pursed her lips deliberately as if to show she wasn't going to talk.

—You don't need to answer, he smiled. Just as your gift for attraction is working on me ... You know, he said simply, that the two of us are attractive as man and woman.

Lóri, already warmed by the whiskey, smiled at such frankness.

—You smiled! Do you know what happened to you? You smiled without shame! Oh, Lóri, when you learn, you'll see how much time you've lost. The tragedy of life does exist and we regret it. But that doesn't keep us from having a deep nearness with joy through that same life.

—I can't! Lóri almost shouted, I can't, I'm lost. If I try to draw nearer to whatever you're talking about I'll be bewildered forever.

He didn't reply, as if she hadn't spoken. They sat in silence until she herself felt she'd pulled herself together.

—I'm not here because I want to give you lessons, unless perhaps for other reasons, because I too am still learning, with difficulty. But there are already so many tired people. My joy is rough and effective, and not smug, it's revolutionary. Anyone can have this joy but they're too busy being lambs of gods.

Though it was fall it was one of the hottest days of the year, Lóri was sweating so much that the back of her dress was soaking, beads of sweat were pearling on her forehead and running down her cheeks. It seemed she was fighting one-on-one against this man, as she was fighting herself, and that it was symbolic that she was sweating and he wasn't. She wiped her face with a tissue, while feeling that Ulisses was scrutinizing her and she realized he was enjoying looking at her. He said:

—In a way you're beautiful. I like your sweaty face without makeup though I also like the over-the-top way you do yourself up. But that's because when you're done up you're proving somehow that you're not a virgin. No, don't get me wrong, don't think I wish you were a virgin, anyway you are somehow. How many men was it you've had?

—Five, she replied knowing perfectly well he hadn't forgotten.

—You know, don't you, that as long as I'm just your friend, I've been sleeping with other women. I was with one for half a year.

—I thought so, she replied without jealousy.

She'd never been jealous of her men but she knew she might become violently jealous of Ulisses, if they became lovers.

—If you become mine one day, the way I want, I'd like to have a child with you, just like this, your unmade face covered in sweat.

She was a little shocked by the unexpected comment, he smiled:

—Don't be afraid. Firstly, because the way I want you to be mine, will only happen when you also want it in the same way. And that will take time because you haven't discovered whatever you need to discover. And what's more, if you do become mine in that way, you might want a child. Because besides constructing ourselves, we'll probably want to construct another being. Lóri, despite my apparent sureness, I too am working to get ready for you. Including from now on, until you're mine, by not going to bed with any other woman.

—No! she exclaimed.

—That doesn't put you under any obligation, silly girl, he laughed. This problem is all mine. And no doubt you've got the wrong idea about men: they can be chaste, Lóri, when they want to be.

Her eyes had taken on a dreamy, distracted look, a bit empty. She was thinking: if Ulisses wanted her to realize something or other in order to become some kind of initiate in life, it would have to happen slowly, if it were quick something in her might be struck down. But she was aware that Ulisses knew that too, and she already knew how patient he was. She was the one losing patience and starting to feel a rush of greed.

—Do you want to walk down to Posto 6? asked Lóri, sometimes the fishermen unload their catch around this time.

He examined her for a long instant that she didn't understand, and suddenly with a sigh and a smile said:

—No, I'm sure you don't know. It's too bad people call you Lóri, because your name Loreley is prettier. Do you know who Loreley was?

—Was she someone?

—Loreley is the name of a legendary character in German folklore, sung about in a lovely poem by Heine. The legend says that Loreley would seduce fishermen with her songs and they'd end up dying at the bottom of the sea, I can't remember the details anymore. No, don't look at me with those guilty eyes. First of all, I'm the one doing the seducing. I know, I know you get all dressed up for me, but that's because I'm seducing you. And I'm not a fisherman, I'm a man who you'll realize one day knows less than he seems to, though he's lived and studied a lot. Now that your eyes are normal (!) again, we can go watch the fishermen, though given how hot it is I had thought of going to dinner with you in Tijuca Forest. But doing both would be too much for you. Lóri, you're waking up through curiosity, that curiosity that drives you into real life. But don't be afraid of the dislocation that will come. That dislocation is needed so you can see everything that, if it were joined up and harmonious, couldn't be seen, would be taken for granted. The dislocation involves a clash between you and reality, you should be prepared for that, Lóri, the truth is that I'm telling you about part of the journey I've already been on. In the worst moments, remember: whoever can suffer intensely, can also feel intense joy. If you want to see the fish, Loreley, let's go.

He paid the check, they got up and started to walk since they weren't far from Posto 6.

They were walking slowly in the breeze that was now blowing in from the sea, and chatting every so often like old friends.

—I wonder if the restaurant in Tijuca Forest still serves chicken in black sauce, nice and black because of the thick blood they use there. When I think of our voracious pleasure in eating the blood of others, I realize how cruel we are, said Ulisses.

—I like it too, Lóri said quietly. Me of all people who could never kill a chicken, I like them so much alive, darting around with their ugly necks and looking for worms. Wouldn't it be better, if we go there, to eat something else? she asked somewhat shaken.

—Of course we should eat it, we mustn't forget and should respect the violence inside us. Small acts of violence save us from greater ones. Maybe, if we didn't eat animals, maybe we'd eat people in their own blood. Our life is cruel, Loreley: we're born with blood and with blood the possibility of perfect union is cut forever: the umbilical cord. And many are they who die from blood spilled inside or out. We must believe in blood as an important part of life. Cruelty is love too.

They were almost there. Ulisses said:

—You walk, Loreley, as if carrying a jug on your shoulder and raising one hand to keep your balance. You're a very ancient woman, Loreley. It doesn't matter that your clothes and hair are in fashion, you're ancient. And it's rare to meet a woman who hasn't broken from the lineage of women down through time. Are you a priestess, Loreley? he asked with a smile.

The good thing, she thought, was that he said disturbing things but immediately cut through the seriousness, which would have upset her, with a smile or an ironic word.

They reached Posto 6 and there was still some light. For the discovery of what Ulisses wanted and which might be called the discovery of living, Lóri preferred the fresh and timid light that came before day or the almost luminous twilight that comes before the night.

Yes, the fish were already there, piled up, silvery, their scales flashing, but their bodies bent by death. The fishermen kept emptying new nets onto the sand where the fish were still squirming almost dead. And from them came the strong sensual smell that raw fish has. Lóri inhaled deeply that almost bad, almost great smell. Only the person herself can express to herself the inexpressible smell of raw fish—not in words: the only way of expressing it is to feel it once again. And, she thought, and to feel the great urge to live more profoundly which that smell would awaken in her. Maybe, she mused, she came from a line of Loreleys for whom the sea and the fishermen were the song of life and death. Only another person who had experienced it would know what she was feeling, since almost everything that matters can't be spoken of. Lóri would have liked to tell Ulisses how the tangy smell of the sea also reminded her of the smell of a healthy man, but she'd never dare. She inhaled again the violently scented and living death of the bluish fish, but the sensation was stronger than she could stand and, at the same time, as she was feeling an extraordinarily nice sensation of being on the verge of fainting from love, she also felt, now out of self-defense, an emptying of herself:

—Let's go, she said almost roughly.

—I warned you, Ulisses said rather severely, that you'd have to be prepared for things to be ruptured. You're wanting to "cut corners," skip the necessary stages and head voraciously into something, whatever it may be. Would you like me to take you home or did you bring money for a cab?

—I did.

—Then go home, Loreley. Farewell.

A LONG AND GLOOMY WINTER FOLLOWED, SO LÓRI read to the children during class and they understood why the cold was wrapping them up in themselves and there was no way to fight it: almost all the children were poor and didn't have enough warm clothes. Lóri used her father's allowance to buy a thick woolen sweater for every pupil in her class, and all were red to heat up their view as well as to stop their lips going purple from the cold which was also coming through the cement floor, in that winter that was colder than other winters, Lóri would come in, she herself dressed warmly like the children, there were multiple voices in the room, she'd teach secure in the knowledge that the boys and girls would retain what she was teaching them for later, when they could understand it. So she told them that arithmetic came from "arithmos" which means rhythm, that number came from "nomos" which means "law" or "norm," norm from the child's universal flow. It was too early to tell them all that, but she took pleasure in saying it, she wanted them to know, through their Portuguese class, that the taste of a fruit is in the contact of the fruit with the palate and not in the fruit itself.

There was no apprenticeship for new things: it was only rediscovery. And it was raining a lot that winter. So she used another allowance from her father and looked for—what pleasure to wander through the shops looking until she found—and looked for and bought red umbrellas and red woolen socks for all her boys and girls.

That was how she was setting the world on fire.

Ulisses rarely looked up. On the phone, but not by way of justifying his behavior, he said that his class that year was exceptional, that it was asking for answers to everything, and that it was forcing him to get down to the hard pleasure of thinking more and studying more.

But one Saturday morning, while she was lying in bed without the courage to face the temperature outside the sheets, the phone rang. She leapt out of bed, but femininely let the phone ring a few times, as she always did in order not to look too eager, in case it were Ulisses.

It was Ulisses and he asked if she'd like to have lunch in Tijuca Forest. She forced herself not to shout yes. Dissembling, she said:

—Today?

—I'll come by in the car at one.

She didn't even need to think about what to wear, she already knew so well: she'd go in her plaid woolen skirt and the red sweater she'd bought for herself too, when she was buying them for the children. She wouldn't need her own red umbrella, since Ulisses was picking her up at the door. Which was too bad. Her red umbrella when it was open looked like a scarlet bird with transparent wings wide open. So she decided to go out at a quarter to one, to wait for him with her red umbrella open.

And that's how he found her and looked at her with wonder: she was extravagant and beautiful.

In silence they drove through the streets until they reached the forest, whose trees were more vegetal than ever, enormous, wrapped in vines, covered with parasites. And when the organic density of the plants and high grasses and trees seemed to be closing in, they arrived at the clearing with the restaurant, lit up because it was such a dark day.

They still hadn't spoken. He took her to a room where a fire was burning in the hearth, then went to order in the main dining room. Soon he was already coming back, he himself holding two glasses of red wine.

—Look, he said, there on the windowsill, a swallow that's split away from its flock.

Its black had a gleam to it shot through with shimmering green, and its breast and the underside of its wings were white. It was perched on the tiled sill of the window.

—Swallows, he said, emigrate and then return, like seagulls. It's unusual to see one alone. This one has split away from its flock, but surely knows where to find it.

And he'd hardly spoken when a bird flew into the room as if crazed for having inadvertently flown through the window, scaring the swallow and scaring itself in the hot prison of the room where it was flying around without knowing where to stop.

—That's a sabiá that's flown its nest, he said, to look for food.

She saw that the sabiá was darker on its wings and had a yellowish breast. But it wasn't singing. Maybe it was a female.

Slowly drinking their wine, they were waiting for their

waiter to tell them lunch was ready. The two of them were the only guests, nobody else seemed to have ventured out in the cold and the drizzle that was falling without any letup. Looking at the fire, she said to him:

—Isn't it strange that I've never asked you where you live?

—You're asking now. I live in Rua Conde Lage, in Glória, in a little old house that's been in the family since my great-grandfather's day. It's called Vila Mariana. It has a rusty wrought-iron gate that screeches every time you open it, and then some steps because in Glória the streets all slope up toward Santa Teresa. Do you know where I mean?

—No.

—It's near the Glória clock. When I'm home, I hear every fifteen minutes a kind of translucent ringing from the clock that sings slowly as it marks the time. It's very nice.

—Isn't that a red-light district?

He smiled:

—So you do know things. It is, has been for ages. But its glory days are over. And, in case you were wondering, no prostitute has ever entered Vila Mariana.

Then they were called to table and went into the dining room. He must have phoned beforehand, because the dish of the day was hen in black sauce. They ate and drank in silence, unhurried. It was nice.

Then they returned to the lounge, which was empty, and sat on the sofa in front of the hearth. There he smoked. When she thought about how, besides the cold, the rain was falling as if onto the whole world, she couldn't believe she'd been given so much good. It was the pact between the Earth and something she'd never realized she needed with so much hunger in her soul. It was raining, raining. The flames were blinking.

He, the man, was busy poking the fire. She hadn't even thought to: it wasn't her role, since she had her man for that. Not that she was a tender maiden, yet the man should do his duty.

The most she did was to encourage him once or twice:

—Look, that log isn't burning ...

And he, before she'd even finished her sentence, had himself already noticed the log, since he was her man, and was already poking it. Not at her command since she was the man's woman and would lose her status if she gave him an order. With his right hand he was holding the poker that was making the flames shoot up. His left hand, the free one, was within her reach. Lóri knew she could take it, that he wouldn't refuse; but she didn't take it, because she wanted things "to happen" and not set them in motion herself. She knew the world of people who anxiously hunt down pleasures and don't know how to wait for them to arrive on their own. And it was so tragic: you only had to look around a nightclub, in the half light: it was the search for pleasure that doesn't come by and of itself. She'd only gone with some of her men from the past, maybe two or three times, and hadn't wanted to go back. Because the search for pleasure, when she'd tried it, had been bad water: she'd put her mouth on the tap, which tasted like rust and only gave two or three drops of lukewarm water: it was dry water. No, she'd thought, better real suffering than forced pleasure. She wanted Ulisses's left hand and knew she wanted it, but she did nothing, since she was enjoying the very thing she was needing: being able to have that hand if she stretched out her own.

Oh, and to say that all this would end. That it couldn't last because of its own nature. No, she didn't mean the fire, she meant what she was feeling. What she was feeling never lasted, it would end and might never return. So she pounced on the moment, devoured the fire inside it, and the fire outside was burning gently, burning, flaring. Then, since everything would end, with vivid imagination, she took the man's free hand, and still in her imagination, as she held that hand between hers, all of her was gently burning, burning, flaring.

BECAUSE IT'S IN THE IMPOSSIBLE THAT YOU FIND RE-
ality.

Lóri could bear the struggle because Ulisses, in the struggle
with her, was not her adversary: he was fighting for her.

—Lóri, pain isn't something to worry about. It's part of animal life.

She clenched her jaw, looked at the frozen moon, looked at
the zenith of the heavenly sphere.

He was crushing a leaf that had fallen from the tree above
the bar table. And as if to give her a present of something, he
said:

—Do you know what mesophyll means?

—I've never heard the word, she replied.

—Mesophyll is the fleshy part of the leaf. Hold this one
and feel it.

He held out the leaf to her, Lóri tapped it with sensitive
fingers and crushed its mesophyll. She smiled. It was lovely to
say and touch: mesophyll.

WHY? BUT WHY HADN'T ULISSES CALLED HER FOR more than two weeks? Might he be waiting for her to call him? And no sooner had she imagined taking the initiative, the harsh reply came to her: never.

Why had he abandoned her? Was it forever? Or had he broken the vow of chastity that he had imposed upon himself in order to wait for her? She kept remembering that his last word, after the visit to Tijuca Forest, had been "farewell." But that was how he always said goodbye. As if cutting their tie just like that? And leaving both of them free of one another? Lóri was aware that she was the one who had cut ties all her life, and maybe something in her suggested to others the word "farewell." "To abandon me right when I was ...," she didn't finish her thought with a sentence because she wasn't sure what "she was ..."

Sometimes at night she'd wake with a start, missing Ulisses, as if she'd once slept with him. And she couldn't get back to sleep because the desire to be possessed by him was too strong. So she'd get up, make coffee, sit like a good girl in a chair with a big cup of coffee. Yet she knew that her intense desire for him still didn't mean she'd made any progress. Because in the past she'd also desired her lovers and hadn't bound herself to any of them.

She was drinking her coffee, and seeing the mute phone beside her. Mute, but also close by if she dared call him. She knew that if she showed him in any way that she already desired him too much, he'd see it was just desire and refuse. And for now she had nothing to give him, except her own body. No, maybe not even her body: for when she'd had lovers it was as if she were only loaning her body to herself for the pleasure, just that, and nothing more.

She was drinking her coffee and thinking without words: my God, and to say that the night is full and that I'm full of the thick night that is dripping with the perfume of sweet almonds. And to think that the world is all thick with so much almond scent, and that I love Thee, God, with a love made of darkness and flashes. And to think that the children of the world grow up and become men and women, and that the night will be full and thick for them too, while I shall be dead, full too. I love Thee, God, without expecting anything but pain from Thou. Pain is the mystery. One of my former pupils who is fifteen by now had bought a carnation to put it in his buttonhole and go to a party. A party, my God, the world is a party that ends in death and in the scent of a wilted carnation in a buttonhole. I love you, God, precisely because I don't know if you exist. I want a sign that you exist. I knew an ordinary woman who didn't ask herself questions about God: she loved beyond the question about God. So God existed. When I die I want carnations attached to my white dress. But not jasmine, which I love so much and which would suffocate my death. After my death I'll only wear white. And I'll meet the one I want: the person I want will also be wearing white.

And sometimes she'd nod off with her hand resting on the table, on the coffee cup.

That was when she entered a phase—was it a phase or forever?—in which she went backward as if she'd lost everything she'd gained. And really—she was wondering ungratefully—what had she gained? Nothing, she replied with hate, she didn't know why, for Ulisses.

God, yes: she'd gained in a new way: loving his impersonal vastness and only wanting Him to exist. But she was starting to lose this too: now she was violently rejecting a God she couldn't plead with. But she also didn't want to plead to Him: she was lost and confused. She remembered that she'd asked Ulisses one day:

—Do you believe in the God?

He'd laughed:

—You're still stuck on those teenage questions? The question is childish. This is the answer: I feel that I am not moving through life inside an absolute emptiness precisely because I too am God. One day, when I can be bothered and if you're still interested, I'll tell you how I move inside God.

Recalling it now, she was surprised to see Ulisses as a stranger to her, a different being, as if she no longer knew him so well. She remembered that he'd added in order to conclude the discussion about God:

—In any case, he'd said in an impersonal way, as if not speaking of himself, I'm one of those people who believe in the unbelievable. I learned to live with whatever can't be understood.

She thought that Ulisses wasn't telling her anything and kept calmly contradicting himself: which made him, in her eyes, the model of a human being. He'd write poems because it was the most profound exercise of man. And what about her? What did she do as a profound exercise of being a person? She did the sea in the morning … In the past she didn't go to the beach out of idleness and also because she didn't like crowds. Now she went without any laziness at five in the morning, when the smell of the still unused sea would make her dizzy with joy. The tangy salt air — *maresia*, a feminine word, though for Lóri the salty smell was masculine. She'd go at five in the morning because that was the hour of the sea's great solitude. Sometimes on the sidewalk she'd pass a man walking his dog, no one else. How to explain that the sea was her maternal cradle but that the smell was all masculine? Maybe it was the perfect fusion. Moreover, at dawn, the caps of the waves looked much whiter.

It was to the world of perfumes that Lóri had awoken. When she'd come back from the street at night, she'd pass a nearby house full of night jessamine, which is like jasmine, but stronger. She'd inhale the smell of jessamine which was nocturnal. And the perfume would seem to kill her slowly. She was fighting it, for she sensed that the perfume was stronger than she was, and that in some way she might die of it. Now was the time she was noticing all this. She was an initiate into the world.

Which seemed like a miracle to her. Not that she believed in miracles, she was the type who spends her whole life rolling stones, and not the type for whom pebbles arrive ready, polished, and white. Though she'd always had fleeting visions, real scenes that would vanish, before falling asleep. But she'd mentioned them to Ulisses and he'd explained that it was a very common phenomenon called eidetic images, and which was the ability to project unconscious images into a hallucinatory field.

Miracles, no. But coincidences. She was living off coincidences, living off lines that kept meeting and crossing and, where they crossed, would form a light and instantaneous point, so light and instantaneous that it was mostly made of secret. As soon as she'd spoken of coincidences, she was already speaking of nothing.

But she did possess a miracle. The miracle of the leaves. She'd be walking down the street and the wind would drop one right on her hair: that line of incidence of millions of leaves transformed into the one that was falling, and of millions of people it would happen to her. This would happen so often that she modestly started to consider herself the leaves' chosen one. With fleeting gestures, she'd pluck the leaf from her hair and stow it in her purse, like the tiniest diamond. Until one day, opening her purse, she'd found among the thousands of things she always carried the dry, curled, dead leaf. She'd thrown it away: she wasn't interested in keeping the dead fetish as a souvenir. And also because she knew that new leaves would coincide with her. One day a falling leaf landed on her eyelashes. Right then she saw God as immensely tactful.

With Ulisses she'd taken the first steps toward some thing she hadn't known before. But could she now make progress by herself? At one of their last meetings she'd asked him with an embarrassed smile, trying to hide behind a lightly ironic tone: am I an autodidact? He'd replied:

—I think so. Lots of things you can only have if you're an autodidact, if you have the courage to be. Other things need to be learned and felt by two people. But I'm hoping. Hoping you'll have the courage to be an autodidact despite the dangers, and also hoping you'll want to be two in one. Your mouth, as I've already said, is passionate. And it's through your mouth that you will start to eat the world, and then the darkness of your eyes will not brighten but iridesce.

He didn't call her, she didn't see him: it occurred to her that he'd disappeared so she could learn by herself. But what happened was that she was still so fragile in the world that she almost fell apart and almost went back to square one. And seeing that she could lose everything she'd gained filled her with the rage of a possessed person against the God. She didn't have the courage to be angry with Ulisses because in her anger she'd destroy him inside herself. But she was turning against the God who was indestructible. This is the prayer of someone possessed, she thought. And she was coming to know the hell of passion for the world, through Ulisses. She didn't know what name to give whatever had taken her over or whatever was, with voracity, taking her over except the word passion.

What was that thing that was so violent that it was making her beg herself for mercy? It was the will to destroy, as if she'd been born to destroy. And the moment of destruction would either come or it wouldn't, that depended on whether she could hear herself. The God was hearing, but could she hear herself?

The destructive force still held back and she didn't understand because she was quivering with joy at being capable of such rage. Because she was living. And there was no danger of really destroying anyone or anything because pity was as strong in her as rage: so she wanted to destroy herself as she was the source of that passion.

She didn't want to ask the God to placate her, she loved the God so much that she was afraid to touch Him with her plea, a plea that was burning, her own prayer was so ardent it was dangerous, and might destroy the last image of God inside her, which she still wanted to save.

Yet, He was the only one she could ask to lay His hand on her and risk burning His own.

That same night she'd stammered a prayer to the God and to herself: give my soul relief, let me feel that Thy hand is holding mine, let me feel that death doesn't exist because in truth we are already in eternity, let me feel that loving is not dying, that the surrender of yourself doesn't mean death but life, let me feel a modest and daily joy, let me not beg too much of Thee, because the answer would be as mysterious as the question, let me receive the world without fear, since for this unfathomable world we were created and are ourselves unfathomable, so it is that there is a connection between this mystery of the world and our own, but that connection isn't clear to us as long as we want to understand it, bless me so I can enjoy the bread I eat, the slumber I sleep, let me show charity and patience toward myself, amen.

Suddenly Lóri could no longer take it and called Ulisses:

—What am I doing, it's night and I'm alive. Being alive is killing me slowly, and I'm wide awake in the dark.

There followed a pause, she started to think Ulisses hadn't heard her. Then he said in a calm and soothing voice:

—Stand firm.

When she hung up, the night was humid and the darkness soft, and living meant having a veil covering your hair. So with tenderness she accepted that she was within the mystery of living.

Before going to bed she went onto the balcony: a full moon was sinister in the sky. So she bathed all over in the lunar rays and felt profoundly clean and calm.

She slowly started falling asleep in gentleness, and the night was deep inside. When the night matured the fuller veil of the dawn breeze would come. For the time being, she was delicately alive, sleeping.

A YEAR HAD GONE BY. THE FIRST HEAT OF SPRING, AN-
cient as a first breath. And which made her smile all the time.
Without looking at herself in the mirror, it was a smile that
had the idiocy of angels.

Long before the arrival of the new season came its harbin-
ger: unexpectedly a mildness in the wind, the first softness
in the air. Impossible! Impossible that this softness in the air
wouldn't bring more! says the heart, breaking.

Impossible, echoes the still nippy and fresh warmth of
spring. Impossible that this air won't bring the love of the
world! Repeats the heart that cracks its singed dryness into a
smile. And doesn't even recognize that it's already brought it,
that that is a love. This still-fresh first heat was bringing: everything. Just that, and indivisibly: everything.

And everything was a lot for a suddenly weakened heart
that could only bear the less, could only want the bit by bit.
Today she was feeling, and there was a keen nip to it, a kind
of future memory of today. And to say that she'd never, never
given what she was feeling to anyone or to anything. Had she
given it to herself?

Only to the extent that the poignancy of whatever was good could fit inside such fragile nerves, in such gentle deaths. Ah how she wanted to die. She'd never yet experienced dying—what a path was still open before her. Dying would have the same indivisible poignancy as goodness. To whom would she give her death? Which would be like the first fresh warmth of a new season.

Ah how much easier to bear and understand pain than that promise of spring's frigid and liquid joy. And with such modesty she was awaiting it: the poignancy of goodness.

But never die before really dying: because it was so good to prolong the promise. She wanted to prolong it with such finesse.

Lóri reveled in that finesse, feeding off the better and finer life, since nothing was too good to prepare her for the instant of that new season. She wanted the best oils and perfumes, wanted the best kind of life, wanted the most tender hopes, wanted the best delicate meats and also the heaviest ones to eat, wanted her flesh to break into spirit and her spirit to break into flesh, wanted those fine mixtures—everything that would secretly ready her for those first moments that would come.

Initiated, she foresaw the change of season. And desired the fuller life of an enormous fruit. Inside that fruit that was preparing itself in her, inside that fruit that was succulent, there was room for the lightest of daytime insomnias which was her wisdom of the wakeful animal: a veil of watchfulness, clever enough to do no more than foresee. Ah foreseeing was gentler than the intolerable acuteness of goodness. And she mustn't forget, in the delicate struggle she was engaged in, that the hardest thing to understand was joy.

She mustn't forget that the steepest ascent, and most exposed to the elements, was to smile with joy. And that's why it was what had least fit inside her: the infinite delicacy of joy. So when she'd linger too long inside it and try to possess its airy vastness, tears of exhaustion would well up in her eyes: she was weak when faced with the beauty of what existed and would yet exist.

And she couldn't manage, in this constant training, to seize the first delight of life.

Would she manage this time to grasp the infinitely sweet delight that was like dying? Ah how she worried she wouldn't manage to live the best she could, and thus one day be able at last to die the best she could. How she would worry that someone might not understand that she'd die on the way to spring's giddy bliss. But she wouldn't rush the arrival of that happiness by one instant—because waiting for it while living was her chaste vigil.

Day and night she wouldn't let the candle go out— prolonging it in the best of kind of holding out.

The first fresh heat of spring … but that was love! Happiness gave her a daughter's smile. She'd cut her hair and was out and about looking good. Except the waiting almost no longer fit inside her. It was so nice that Lóri was running the risk of overdoing it, of losing her first springtime death, and, in the sweat of too much clammy waiting, dying too early. Out of curiosity dying too early: since she was already wanting to know what the new season was like.

But she'd wait. She'd wait while eating with delicacy and decorum and controlled avidity each tiniest crumb of everything, wanting everything since nothing was too good for her death which was her life so eternal that this very day it already existed and already was.

Through that world she started to wander. She'd met

Ulisses, in her search she journeyed far into herself. And then finally the day came when she realized she was no longer on her own, recognized Ulisses, had found her destiny as a woman. And to know that he was chaste, waiting for her, she found natural and accepted. For she, despite desire, didn't want to rush anything and remained chaste too.

Everyone was fighting for freedom — that's what she was seeing in the newspapers, and she was happy that injustices were finally no longer being tolerated. In the Sunday paper she saw the lyrics to a song from Czechoslovakia. She copied it out in her best teacher's handwriting, and gave it to Ulisses. It was called "Distant Voice" and went like this:

> Low and far off
> It's the voice I hear. Where from,
> So weak and vague?
> It imprisons me in words,
> I struggle to grasp
> The things it asks about
> I don't and I don't know
> How I'll answer it.
>
> Only the wind knows,
> Only the wise sun can see.
> Thoughtful birds,
> Love is beautiful,
> Suggest something to me.
> And the rest
> Only the wind knows,
> Only the sun can see.

Why, in the distance, do rocks arise,
Why does love come?
People don't care,
Why does everything work out for them?
Why can't I change the world?
Why don't I know how to kiss?
I don't and I don't know
Maybe someday I'll understand.

Only the wind knows,
Only the wise sun can see.
Thoughtful birds,
Beautiful love,
Suggest something to me.
And the rest,
Only the wind knows,
Only the sun can see.

The song's lyrics were by a name that was charming her with its strangeness and she asked Ulisses to pronounce it which he did with ease: Zdenek Rytir. And the music, which she'd never hear, was by Karel Svoboda.

—It's pretty, Loreley, there's a pretty and accepting sadness about it.

Then suddenly she'd calmed down. Never, until then, had she felt the sensation of absolute calm. She was now feeling such a great clarity that it was canceling her out as a simple, existing person: it was an empty lucidity, like a perfect mathematical calculation that you don't need. She was clearly seeing the void. And not even understanding the thing that part of her was understanding. What would she do with this lucidity? She also knew that her clarity could become a human hell. For she knew that—in terms of our daily and permanent resigned accommodation with unreality—clarity of reality was a risk. "And so put out my flame, God, because it is no use to me for my days. Help me once again to consist in a more possible way. I consist, I consist."

In some way she'd already learned that each day was never common, was always extraordinary. And that it was up to her to suffer through or take pleasure in the day. She wanted the pleasure of the extraordinary which was so simple to find in common things: the thing didn't need to be extraordinary in order for her to feel the extraordinary in it.

For days she seemed to meditate deeply but she wasn't meditating on anything: she was only feeling the gentle pleasure, which was also physical, of well-being.

And now she was the one who was feeling the desire to be apart from Ulisses, for a while, to learn on her own how to be. Two weeks had already passed and Lóri would sometimes feel a longing so enormous that it was like a hunger. It would only pass when she could eat Ulisses's presence. But sometimes the longing was so deep that his presence, she figured, would seem paltry; she would want to absorb Ulisses completely. This desire of hers to be Ulisses's and for Ulisses to be hers for a complete unification was one of the most urgent feelings she'd ever had. She got a grip, didn't call, happy she could feel.

But the nascent pleasure would ache so much in her chest that sometimes Lóri would have preferred to feel her usual pain instead of this unwanted pleasure. True joy had no possible explanation, not even the possibility of being understood—and seemed like the start of an irreparable perdition. That merging with Ulisses that had been and still was her desire, had become unbearably good. But she was aware that she still wasn't up to enjoying a man. It was as if death were our great and final good, except it wasn't death, it was unfathomable life that was taking on the grandeur of death. Lóri thought: I can't have a petty life because it wouldn't match the absoluteness of death.

From the minutes of joy she'd gone through, Lóri found out that you should let yourself be flooded bit by bit by joy—since it was life being born. And anyone who wasn't strong enough to have pleasure should cover every nerve with a protective coating, with a coating of death in order to tolerate the mightiness of life. Lóri might have this coating in any formal occasion, in any kind of silence, in school lessons or in a bunch of meaningless words: it was what she did. For you don't toy with pleasure. Pleasure was us.

And inside Lóri pleasure, through a lack of practice, was at the threshold of anguish. Her chest seized up, her strength crumbled: yes, it was anguish. And, if she did nothing to fight it, she was aware that it would be the worst anguish she'd ever felt. Then she grew afraid.

Then she called Ulisses. He answered and, if he'd been surprised, he hadn't shown it. She could barely speak, she was so lost: she'd taken a step beyond pleasure and had frightened herself.

When she finally managed to speak, she said to him:

—Ulisses, I was doing well and suddenly I'm really not.

He said:

—You must have gone too far for a beginner.

She said:

—I don't know if you still plan to see me someday …

He interrupted her with a gentle "but of course, whenever you want."

Everything he'd said—especially the tone he'd used—was meant to soothe her. And she felt so strong through him that, restored and calm again, she said to him:

—I'd rather be on my own for a little longer, even if it's so hard.

—It's a sacrifice for me too. But do as you wish, if that's what you need.

She then spoke with a tranquility she didn't know she had in her:

—It is, Ulisses, it's what I still need.

Once again Ulisses had helped her, especially with the tone of his voice that was so rich in inflections. And Lóri thought that might be one of the most important human and animal experiences: asking mutely for help and mutely that help being given. Because, despite the words, it had been mutely that he'd helped her. Lóri was feeling as if she were a dangerous tiger with an arrow buried in its flesh, and which had been circling slowly around frightened people to see who would take away its pain. And then a man, Ulisses, had felt that a wounded tiger isn't dangerous. And approaching the beast, unafraid to touch her, he had carefully pulled out the buried arrow.

And the tiger? No, neither people nor animals can say thank you for certain things. So she, the tiger, had paced languorously in front of the man, hesitated, licked one of her paws and then, since neither a word or a grunt was what mattered, gone off in silence. Lóri would never forget the help she'd received when she could only manage to stammer with fear.

AND LÓRI CONTINUED IN HER SEARCH FOR THE WORLD.
She went to the fruit and vegetable and fish and flower market: you could get everything at those stalls, full of shouts, of
people jostling, squeezing the produce to see if it was good—
Lóri went to see the abundance of the earth that was brought
each week to a street near her house as an offering to the God
and to men. For her survey of the nonhuman world, in order to make contact with the living neutrality of things that,
while not thinking, were nevertheless living, she would wander
through the stalls and it was hard to get close to any of them,
there were so many women milling about with bags and carts.

At last she saw: pure purple blood running from a crushed
beet root on the ground. But her gaze fell on a basket of potatoes. They had different shapes and nuanced colors. She took
one of them in her two hands, and its round skin was smooth.
The skin of the potato was dusky, and delicate like a newborn's. Although, when she turned it this way and that, she
could feel with her fingers the almost imperceptible presence
of tiny buds, invisible to the naked eye. That potato was very

lovely. She didn't want to buy it because she didn't want to see it shrivel at home and certainly didn't want to cook it.

The potato is born inside the earth.

And this was a joy she learned right there: the potato is born inside the earth. And inside the potato, if you peel it, it is whiter than a peeled apple.

The potato was unsurpassed as food. She realized this, and it was a light hallelujah.

She slipped through the hundreds of people at the market and inside her she had grown. She stopped for a moment at the stall selling eggs.

They were white.

At the fish stand she squinted and once again inhaled the tangy smell of the fish, and the smell was their souls after death.

The pears were so replete with themselves that, in that ripeness they were almost at their peak. Lóri bought one and right there at the market bit into the flesh of the pear which yielded totally. Lóri was aware that only someone who has eaten a succulent pear could understand her. And she bought a kilo. Maybe not to eat at home, just for decoration, and to be able to look at them for a few more days.

As if she were a painter who had just emerged from an abstract phase, now, without becoming figurative, she had entered a new realism. In this realism each thing at the market had its own importance, connected to a whole—but what was the whole? For as long as she didn't know, she turned her attention to objects and shapes, as if whatever existed were part of an exhibition of painting and sculpture. If the object were of bronze—at the stall selling trinkets for presents, she saw the small, badly made bronze statuette—the object of bronze, it almost burned in her hands because she enjoyed handling it so much. She bought a bronze ashtray, because the statuette was too ugly.

And suddenly she saw the turnips. She was seeing everything to the point of filling herself with a plenitude of vision and with her handling of the fruits of the earth. Each fruit was unwonted, though familiar and hers. Most had an exterior that was meant to be seen and recognized. Which delighted Lóri. Sometimes she'd compare herself to the fruits, and despising her external appearance, she'd eat herself internally, full of living juice as she was. She was trying to leave pain, as if trying to leave another reality that had lasted her whole life up to that point.

BUT HER SEARCH WASN'T EASY. HER DIFFICULTY WAS being what she was, which was suddenly turning into an insurmountable difficulty.

One day she sought among the papers strewn throughout the drawers of her house the test written by the best pupil in her class, which she wanted to have another look at in order to give the boy more guidance. And she couldn't find it, though she remembered that, when she'd put it away, she'd been careful not to lose it, since it was a precious piece of writing. She looked in vain. So she wondered, as she had for years, since she often lost the things she kept: if I were I and had to keep an important document where would I put it? Usually this would help her to find the object.

But this time she felt so pressured by the phrase "if I were I" that the hunt for the paper lost importance and she started thinking without wanting to, which for her meant feeling.

And she wasn't feeling comfortable. "If I were I" had made her feel awkward: the lie in which she'd been living so comfortably had just been shifted slightly from the spot where it had settled. Yet she'd read biographies of people who had suddenly become themselves and changed their lives completely, at least their inner lives. Lóri was thinking that if she were she, acquaintances wouldn't greet her on the street because even her countenance would have changed. "If I were I" seemed to represent the greatest danger in living, seemed like another return of the unknown.

At the same time, Lóri had an intuition that, once the early turbulence of the coming intimate celebrations had passed, she'd finally have the experience of the world. She was well aware, she'd finally experience in full the pain of the world. And her own pain as a mortal creature, the pain she'd learned not to feel. But she'd sometimes be swept up by an ecstasy of pure and legitimate pleasure that she could scarcely imagine. Though actually she was starting to imagine it because she felt herself smiling and also felt the kind of bashfulness you feel in the face of something that is too big. To be what you are was too big and uncontrollable. Lóri was feeling a kind of hesitation about going too far. She'd always held back a bit as if gripping the reins of a horse that could gallop off and take her God knows where. She was keeping herself back. Why and for what? What was she saving herself for? It was a certain fear of her capabilities, strong or weak. Maybe she was containing herself out of the fear of not knowing a person's limits.

Two days later Ulisses called her and asked if she still needed to be alone. She replied, holding back her despair and holding back the desire to fall into his arms so he could protect her, she replied: I still do.

Her despair came from not even knowing where and how to start. She only knew that she'd started a new thing and could never return to her former dimensions. And she also knew that she should start modestly, in order not to get discouraged. And she knew that she should abandon forever the main road. And go down her true path which was the narrow byways.

It was the next day when as she was walking slowly and tiredly down the street, she saw the girl standing and waiting for a bus. And her heart started to beat—because she'd decided to try to make contact with a person. She stopped.

—Is the bus late? she asked, shy and a little disoriented.

—Yes.

She'd failed. Her heart beat even louder because she felt she wasn't going to give up.

—Your dress is really pretty. I like that big purple print.

The girl smiled immediately.

—I bought it in a shop, and it was cheaper than if I'd had it made. My seamstress is a nightmare, with each dress she gets more expensive, and that's not counting the notions I pay extra for. So I think—

Lóri didn't hear anything more: she kept smiling blissfully: she'd made contact with a stranger. She interrupted her somewhat brusquely but with a grateful sweetness in her voice:

—Goodbye. Thank you, thank you very much.

The girl replied in surprise:

—Don't you want to know where I bought it?

—There's no need, thank you.

She still managed to glimpse the girl's astonishment. She kept walking. No, that wasn't the right type of contact. Deeper contact was what mattered. When she got home she called Ulisses:

—What should I do? I can't bear living. Life is so short and I can't bear living.

—But there's so much, Lóri, that you still don't know. And there's a place where despair is a light and a love.

—And afterward?

—Afterward is Nature.

—You're calling death Nature.

—No, Lóri, I'm calling us Nature.

—Can it be that all lives were like this?

—I don't know, Lóri.

Again, since he hadn't feared the wounded tiger and had pulled out the arrow buried in its body. Oh God! Having just one life was so little!

Love for Ulisses came like a wave that she'd managed to hold back until then. But suddenly she was no longer wanting to hold it back.

And when she realized she was accepting love in full, her joy was so great that her heart started beating all through her body, it seemed to her as if a thousand hearts were beating in the depths of her person. A right-to-be possessed her, as if she'd just finished crying after being born. How? How to stretch birth out for a whole lifetime? She quickly went to the mirror to find out who Loreley was and to find out if she could be loved. But she got a shock when she saw herself.

I exist, I see that, but who am I? And she was afraid. It seemed to her that by feeling less pain, she'd lost the advantage of pain as a warning and symptom. She'd become incomparably more serene but in mortal danger: she could be a step from the death of her soul, a step from its already having died, and without the benefit of her own advance warning.

In her fright she called Ulisses. And his domestic said he wasn't there. So every fifteen minutes, with her fear and pain unleashed, she'd call him. Until two hours later, he himself answered the phone:

—Ulisses, I can't find an answer when I wonder who I am. I know a bit about me: I am the one who has my own life and yours too, I drink your life. But that doesn't answer who I am!

—There's no answer to that, Lóri. Don't pretend you're strong enough to ask the worst question. I myself still can't ask who I am without getting lost.

And his voice had sounded like a lost man's. Lóri was astounded. No, no, she wasn't lost, she was even going to make a list of things she could do!

She sat with a blank page and wrote: eat—look at fruit in the market—see people's faces—feel love—feel hate—have something not known and feel an unbearable suffering—wait impatiently for the beloved—sea—go into the sea—buy a new swimsuit—make coffee—look at objects—listen to music—holding hands—irritation—be right—not be right and give in to someone who is—be forgiven for the vanity of living—be a woman—do myself credit—laugh at the absurdity of my condition—have no choice—have a choice—fall asleep—but of bodily love I shall not speak.

After the list she still didn't know who she was, but she knew a great many things she could do.

And she knew that she was a fierce one among fierce human beings, we, monkeys of ourselves. We'd never reach the human being inside ourselves. And whoever did was rightly called a saint. Because to relinquish ferocity was a sacrifice. Which apostle was it who'd said of us: you are gods?

She remembered a conversation she'd had with Ulisses and in which he'd wondered almost absentmindedly:

—God isn't intelligent, you see, because He is Intelligence. He is the sperm and egg of the cosmos that includes us. But I'd like to know why you, instead of saying God, like everyone else, say the God?

—Because God is a noun.

—There's the primary school teacher talking.

—No, He is a noun, substantive like substance. There's no single adjective for the God.

"You are gods." But we were gods with adjectives.

IT WAS THE NEXT DAY WHEN COMING INSIDE THAT she saw the single apple on the table.

It was a red apple, with a smooth tough skin. She took the apple in both hands: it was fresh and heavy. She replaced it on the table in order to see it as before. And it was as if she were seeing the photo of an apple in empty space.

After examining it, turning it over, seeing as never before its roundness and its scarlet color—then slowly, she took a bite.

And, oh God, as if it were the forbidden apple of paradise, but this time she knew good, and not just evil as before. Unlike Eve, when she bit the apple she entered paradise.

She just took a bite and put the apple back down on the table. Because some unknown thing was gently happening. It was the start—of a state of grace.

Only someone who has been in grace, could recognize what she was feeling. It wasn't an inspiration, which was a special grace that so often happens to people who work in art.

The state of grace she was in wasn't used for anything. It was as if it came just to let you know you really existed. In this state, besides the tranquil happiness that would shine from people remembered and from things, there was a lucidity that Lóri was only describing as light in weight because in grace everything was so, so light. It was a lucidity of someone who's no longer guessing: who, without effort, knows. Just that: knows. Don't ask what, since the person could only answer in the same childish way: without effort, you know.

And there was a physical beatitude to which nothing could be compared. The body was transforming itself into a gift. And she felt that it was a gift because she was experiencing, from a direct source, the unquestionable blessing of existing materially.

In the state of grace, you can see the profound beauty, once unreachable, of another person. Everything, in fact, acquired a kind of halo that was not imaginary: it came from the splendor of the almost mathematical radiance of things and of people. You'd start to feel that everything that exists—person or thing—was breathing and exhaling a kind of fine sheen of energy. That energy is the world's greatest truth and is impalpable.

Not in the slightest could Lóri imagine what the state of grace of the saints must be. She had never known that state and couldn't even guess at it. What was happening to her was just the state of grace of an average person who suddenly becomes real, because she is average and human and recognizable and has eyes and ears to see and hear.

The discoveries in that state were unutterable and incommunicable. She remained seated, quiet, silent. It was like an annunciation. It wasn't however preceded by the angels who, she assumed, would come before the grace of the saints. But it was as if the angel of life were coming to announce to her the world.

Afterward she slowly came out of that situation. Not as if she'd been in a trance—there hadn't been a trance—she was emerging slowly, with a sigh of someone who had the world as it is. It was also already a sigh of longing. Because having experienced gaining a body and a soul and the earth and the sky, you want more and more. But there was no point desiring it: it would only come spontaneously.

Lóri couldn't explain why, but she thought that animals entered the grace of existing more often than humans. Except they didn't know, and humans realized it. Humans had obstacles that didn't get in the way of animals' lives, like reason, logic, understanding. While animals had the splendor of something that is direct and moves directly.

The God knew what he was doing: Lóri thought it was right that the state of grace wasn't given to us often. If it were, we might pass once and for all to the "other side" of life, which other side was real too but nobody would ever understand us: we'd lose the common language.

It was also good that it didn't come as much as you'd like: because she could get used to happiness. Yes, because you're very happy in a state of grace. And to get used to happiness, that would be a social danger. We'd get more selfish, because happy people are, less sensitive to human pain, we wouldn't feel the necessity to try to help those in need—all because in grace we have understanding, and the sum of life.

No, even were it up to Lóri, she wouldn't often want to have the state of grace. It would be like falling prey to an addiction, it would attract her like an addiction, she'd become as contemplative as users of opium. And if it appeared more often, Lóri was sure she'd take advantage of it: she'd start to want to live permanently in grace. And that would represent an unforgivable escape from human destiny, which was made of struggle and suffering and confusion and joys.

It was also good that the state of grace lasted only a few moments. If it lasted longer, she was well aware, she who knew her almost childlike ambitions, she'd end up trying to enter the mysteries of Nature. As soon as she tried, moreover, she was sure that grace would disappear. For grace was a blessing and, if it demanded nothing, it would vanish if we asked it for an answer. You couldn't forget that the state of grace was just a small opening onto the world that was a kind of paradise — but it wasn't like a way in, nor did it give you the right to eat of the fruit of its orchards.

Lóri emerged from the state of grace with a smooth face, her eyes open and thoughtful and, though she hadn't smiled, it was as if her whole body had just emerged from a gentle smile. And had emerged a better creature than had gone in.

She'd experienced some thing that seemed to redeem the human condition, though at the same time the narrow limits of that condition were accentuated. And exactly because after grace the human condition was revealing itself in all its imploring poverty, you learned to love more, hope more. You'd start to have a kind of trust in suffering and in its so often unbearable paths.

There were days that were so arid and desolate that she'd give years of her life in exchange for a few minutes of grace.

TWO DAYS LATER ULISSES CALLED AND THIS TIME HE seemed to be demanding her presence, as if he could no longer bear to wait.

She went. As she was approaching Ulisses, who was sitting at the terrace of the bar drinking, he looked at her coming over and out of so much disappointed surprise didn't even get up:

—But you cut your hair! You should have asked me first!

—I hadn't planned to, I just did.

She knew how he was feeling because she'd had an excruciating sense of loss as her hair was cut and the dead locks were falling to the floor.

—I'm going to let it grow out again but long enough to make braids I can tie above my forehead.

He agreed but was disappointed. Lóri observed him: he was looking tired. And she guessed that his fatigue was also coming from the wait she'd forced him to have.

—Ulisses, remember how you once asked me why I voluntarily kept away from people? Now I can tell you. It's because I don't want to be platonic in relation to myself. I'm profoundly defeated by the world I live in. I separated myself just for a while because of my defeat and because I felt that other people were defeated too. So I closed myself up in an individualization that if I hadn't been careful could have been transformed into a hysterical or contemplative solitude. What saved me were always my pupils, the children. You know, Ulisses, they're poor and that's why the school doesn't require uniforms. In the winter I bought them each a red sweater. Now, for spring, I'm going to buy the boys blue shirts and trousers, and the girls blue dresses. Or maybe I'll order them, that might be easier. I'll have to get all the pupils' measurements because—

The one who got up to leave was Ulisses, to Lóri's surprise. He said:

—You're ready, Lóri. Now I want what you are, and you want what I am. And the whole exchange will happen in bed, Lóri, at my house and not at your apartment. I'm going to write my address on this napkin. You know when I'm teaching and when I give private lessons. Outside of those hours, I'll be home waiting for you. I'll fill my bedroom with roses, and if they wilt before you come, I'll buy new roses. You can come whenever you want. If I'm in the middle of a private lesson, you'll wait. If you want to come in the middle of the night and are afraid of taking a taxi by yourself, call and I'll come get you.

As he was speaking, he was writing his address on the napkin, calling the waiter, and paying the bill. He held out the napkin to Lóri who took it, terrified.

—Lóri, I won't call you again. Until you come on your own. I'd rather you not call to let me know you're coming. I'd like you, without a word, just to come.

It was liberty he was offering her. Though she'd rather he order her around, set a day and time. But she felt there was no point in trying to make him change his mind. At the same time she was happy just to go to his house whenever she wanted. Because, suddenly, she was determined never to go. For they had reached a maturity in their relations, and she was afraid that sleeping together in a bed would break the spell.

During the first days Lóri was bothered because she was sure Ulisses was waiting. It pained her for the roses to wilt and for him pathetically to replace them with others that would wilt too. It consoled her to think that his wait wouldn't be too painful for him, since he was an extremely patient man who was capable of suffering. So she calmed down. She thought now that the ability to bear suffering was the measure of a person's greatness and saved that person's inner life.

Over the next days she was much helped in passing the time because she'd brought home the exam papers for marking.

Besides she was full and didn't need anyone, it was enough to know that Ulisses loved her and that she loved him. Moreover she was enveloped in a new love for things and people. For things: she bought a green glass vase and painted it an opaque white and that way the flowers she'd buy at the market would leap out of the white. She bought a soapstone ashtray, and couldn't resist: with her nail she scratched the bottom of it, marking it, engraving it. And she bought a white dimity dress: if she went to see Ulisses, she'd wear this dress. As for people, she was being sincerely sweet and joyous with the pupils whom she now loved with a mother's love.

One night she called her friend the fortune-teller and said she was coming over. She didn't much care what the fortune-teller would tell her about the future and a certain love. What she cared most about was this: she'd seen a Thing. It was ten at night in Praça Tiradentes and the taxi was going fast. Then she saw a street she'd never forget. She wasn't even planning to describe it: that street was hers. She could only say that it was empty and that it was ten at night. Nothing more. She had however, been germinated.

A FEW NIGHTS LATER SHE WAS SLEEPING. AND THOUGH it sounds like a contradiction, softly all of a sudden the pleasure of being asleep had awoken her with a gentle start. She stayed lying down for a while and was still feeling the taste in her whole body of that rural area where, underground, she had spread from the roots the tentacles of some dream. It most definitely, by the way, was a good dream that had woken her.

She got up and went to drink a glass of water, without wanting to turn on the lights, trying to get oriented in the darkness which wasn't total because of the strong light from the house next door. It was only eleven at night. Since she'd gone to bed at ten, she'd only slept an hour, woken by the pleasure of sleeping.

She went to drink the water slowly on the terrace. She felt by the smell of the air and the restlessness of the branches of the trees that it would soon rain. You couldn't see the moon. The air was muggy, there was a strong smell of jasmine coming from the neighbor's jasmine bush. Lóri stood on the terrace, somewhat suffocated by the intense perfume. Through the drunkenness of the jasmine, for a moment a revelation came to her, in the form of a feeling—and in the next instant she'd forgotten whatever she'd learned from the revelation. It was as if the pact with the God were this: see and forget, in order not to be struck down by the unbearable knowledge.

Standing there, softer than before, in the semidarkness of the terrace, another revelation came to her that lasted longer because it was the intuitive result of things she'd previously thought rationally. What came to her was the slightly shocking certainty that our feelings and thoughts are as supernatural as a story that takes place after death. And she didn't understand what she meant by that. She let it linger, the thought, because she knew it was covering another, more profound and more comprehensible. Simply, with the glass of water in her hand, she was discovering that thinking wasn't natural for her. Then she reflected a little, with her head cocked to one side, on how she didn't have a day-to-day. It was a life-to-life. And that life was supernatural.

At that hour of the night she was experiencing that fear of being alive, having as her only help the helplessness of being alive. Life was so strong that it was helping itself through its own helplessness. Being alive—she felt—she would from now on make her motive and theme. With gentle curiosity, enveloped in the scent of jasmine, attentive to the hunger of existence, and attentive to her own attention, she seemed to be eating delicately alive what was very much hers. The hunger of living, my God. How far she was going in the wretchedness of need: she'd exchange an eternity after death for eternity while she was alive.

Until she really was hungry, she fetched a pear and came back to the terrace. She was eating. Her human soul was the only possible way of not crashing disastrously into her physical organization, it was such a perfect machine. Her human soul was also the only way given to her to accept without madness the general soul of the world. If the gears failed for half a fraction of a second, she'd fall into nothing.

Despite the threat of looming rain and of the anguish the suffocating jasmine was already giving her, she was discovering, discovering. And it wasn't raining, wasn't raining. But the darkest hour preceded that thing that she didn't even want to try to define. That thing was a light inside her, and people would call it joy, tame joy.

She felt a bit bewildered as if a heart had been pulled out of her, and in its place was now a sudden absence, an almost palpable absence, of something that before had been an organ bathed in the darkness of pain.

Because she was feeling the great pain. In that pain however was the opposite of a numbness: it was a lighter and more silent way to exist. Who am I? she wondered in great danger. And the smell of the jasmine bush replied: I am my perfume.

She saw that, like the restless swaying of the neighbor's trees, she too was indocile, restless. She'd organized herself in order to console herself for the anguish and pain. But how do you find consolation from the mixture of simple and calm joy with anguish? She wasn't used to doing without consolation.

Then it finally started to rain.

First a drizzle, then so heavy that it made noise on all the rooftops.

I get it, she suddenly thought. She realized that she was seeking in the rain a joy so great that it became acute, which would put her in touch with an acute feeling like the acuteness of pain. But the search had been pointless. She was at the terrace door and all that was happening was this: she was seeing the rain and the rain was falling in harmony with her. She and the rain were busy flowing with violence.

How long would this state of hers last? She noticed that with this question she was taking her pulse in order to feel where the earlier painful pounding might be.

And she saw that there was no pounding pain as before. Just this: it was pouring rain and she was seeing the rain and getting soaked.

What simplicity.

She'd never imagined that the world and she would ever reach this point of ripe wheat. The rain and Lóri were as joined as the water of the rain was to the rain. And she, Lóri, wasn't giving thanks for anything. Hadn't she, just after birth taken by chance and necessity the path she'd taken—which?—and wouldn't she have always been what she now was really being: a peasant who is in a field where it's raining. Not even thanking the God or Nature. The rain wasn't giving thanks for anything either. Without gratitude or ingratitude. Lóri was a woman, she was a person, a watchfulness, an inhabited body looking at the thick rain fall. As the rain wasn't grateful for not being hard like a rock: she was the rain. Maybe she was this, exactly this: living. And despite just living she was full of a tame joy, that of a horse that eats from your hand. Lóri was tamely happy.

And suddenly, but without a fright, she felt an extreme urge to give this secret night to someone. And that someone was Ulisses. Her heart started to pound, and she felt pale because all her blood, she felt, had drained from her face, all because she felt so suddenly Ulisses's desire and her own desire. She stood there for a moment, for one unbalanced moment. Then her heart pounded even faster and louder because she realized she wouldn't put it off any longer, it would be tonight.

She got from her bag his address written on the napkin, put her raincoat over her short nightdress, and in the coat pocket put some money. And without any makeup on her face, with what was left of her short hair falling over her forehead and neck, she went out to hail a cab. It had all been so quick and intense that she hadn't even thought to change out of her nightdress, or put on her makeup.

MAYBE OUT OF A NEED TO PROTECT THAT TOO-YOUNG soul, in him and in her, he without humiliating himself, but with unexpected devotion and also begging mercy so they wouldn't hurt each other in this first birth—maybe for all those reasons he knelt before her. And for Lóri that was very nice. Especially because she was aware that it was nice for him too—it was after covering great distances that a man would finally understand that he needed to kneel before his woman as if before his mother. And for Lóri it was nice because the man's head was close to her knees and close to her hands, in her lap which was her hottest part. And she could make her best gesture: with hands that were both quivering and firm, take that tired head which was her fruit and his. That man's head belonged to that woman.

Never had a human been closer to another human being. And Lóri's pleasure was finally opening her hands and letting slip away without greed the full-emptiness that before had so fiercely been grasping her. And suddenly the surge of joy: she noticed that she was opening her hands and her heart but that she could do so without danger! I'm not losing anything! I'm finally giving myself and what happens when I'm giving myself is that I receive, receive. Careful, is there a danger in the heart's being free?

She realized, while gently stroking the man's dark hair, she realized that in this spreading-out of hers was contained the still-dangerous pleasure of being. Yet a strange security was coming too: it came from the sudden certainty that she'd always have something to spend and give. So there was no more greed with her full-emptiness that was her soul, and she'd spend it in the name of a man and of a woman.

— Tonight seems like a dream to me.

— But it's not. It's that reality is unbelievable.

— What's that bell ringing?

— It's the Glória clock that rings every fifteen minutes with chimes that terrify the pigeons.

Lóri had only one fear: that Ulisses, the great Ulisses whose head she was holding, would let her down. Like her father who had overburdened her with contradictions: he had turned her, his daughter, into his protector. And she, in her childhood, couldn't even look at her father when he was happy about something, because he, the strong one, the wise one, became in his joys entirely innocent and so disarmed. Oh God, her father would forget for a few moments that he was mortal. And would make her, a girl, shoulder the weight of the responsibility of knowing that our most naive and most animal pleasures would die too. In those instants when he'd forget he was going to die, he would turn her, a girl, into a Pietà, the mother of men.

But with Ulisses it felt different now. He'd never been humble in love, out of wonder, he was becoming humble. She didn't realize how, there on his knees, he'd got her to kneel beside him on the floor, without her feeling awkward. And once the two were kneeling he finally kissed her.

He kissed her for a long time until both could let go, and they sat looking each other in the eye without shame. They both knew they'd already gone too far. And they were still feeling the danger of surrendering so totally. They remained silent. That was when lying on the floor they loved each other so deeply that they were scared of their own greatness.

—Slowly, Lóri, slowly, we have the whole night, slowly.

They seemed to understand that when love was too big and when one person couldn't live without the other, this love was no longer applicable: nor could the beloved receive so much. Lóri was confused to notice that even in love you had to keep your common sense and sense of proportion. For an instant, as if they'd planned it, he kissed her hand, humanizing himself. For there was the danger of, in a manner of speaking, dying of love.

And as soon as the danger passed, he kissed her again without any fear.

—What was sex like for you before?

—It was the only thing, she said, that I got right.

—I suspected as much, he said, and out of pure jealousy, he hurt her: when I saw you in the street the first time I immediately saw you'd be good in a bed.

Lóri's peasant vitality is what saved her from a world of excessively delicate emotions. He saw that he'd hurt her out of jealousy. And said:

—But tonight is my first time.

At first he'd treated her with delicacy and a willingness to wait as if she were a virgin. But soon Lóri's hunger made

Ulisses forget all courtesy, and it was with a voracity without joy that they loved each other the second time. And if that wasn't enough, since they'd waited so long, almost immediately they really possessed each other again, this time with an austere and silent joy. She felt herself losing all the weight of her body like a figure from Chagall.

Then they lay there quietly, holding hands. For an instant she took her hand away, lit a cigarette, passed it to him, and lit another for herself—and then took his hand again. Soon he stubbed his out. It was dark, the way she'd wanted, and neither spoke a word. I never knew myself like now, Lóri was feeling. It was a knowledge without mercy or joy or blame, it was a realization you couldn't translate into feelings separated from each other and hence without names. It was a vast and calm knowing that "I am not I," she was feeling. And it was also the very least, because it was, at the same time, a macrocosm and a microcosm. I know myself as the larva transmutes into a chrysalis: this is my life between vegetable and animal. She was as complete as the God: except the Latter had a wise and perfect ignorance that guided Him and the Universe. To know herself was supernatural. But the God was natural. Lóri wanted to transmit this to Ulisses but didn't have the gift of words and couldn't explain what she was feeling or thinking, not to mention that she was thinking almost without words.

She guessed that he was about to fall asleep, and so she slowly took her hand out of his. He immediately felt her touch disappear and said half-awake and half-asleep:

—It's because I love you.

So she, in a low voice in order not to wake him completely, said for the first time in her life:

—It's because I love you.

A great peace took hold of her for having finally said it. Unafraid of waking him and unafraid of his answer, she asked:

—Listen, are you still going to want me?

—More than ever, he replied with a calm and controlled voice. The truth, Lóri, is that deep down I've been searching all my life for the intoxication of holiness. I'd never thought that what I'd achieve was the holiness of the body.

As for her, she'd struggled her whole life against a penchant for reverie, never letting it sweep her to the final waters. But the effort of swimming against the sweet current had sapped some of her life force. Now, in the silence in which they both found themselves, she opened her doors, relaxed her soul and body, and didn't realize how much time had passed for she had surrendered to a profound and blind reverie that the Glória clock didn't interrupt.

He stirred in the bed. Then she spoke:

—You once said that when people ask my name I shouldn't say Lóri but "I." Well it's only now that I call myself "I." And say: I am in love with your I. So we is. Ulisses, we is original.

The night was getting darker and darker and it was raining a lot. Though she couldn't see him, she recognized by his measured breathing that he was sleeping. Her eyes were open in the dark and the darkness kept revealing itself to her as a dense compact pleasure, almost unrecognizable as pleasure, when compared to what she'd had with Ulisses. His sleeping beside her, was leaving her both alone and integrated. She didn't want anything except just what was happening to her: to be a woman in the dark beside a man who was sleeping. She wondered for an instant if death could interfere with the heavy pleasure of being alive. And the answer was that not even the idea of death could manage to disturb the boundless dark field in which everything was throbbing thick, heavy and happy. Death had lost its glory.

She remembered how it was before these moments now. She was a woman seeking a way, a form. And now she had what in fact was so much more perfect: it was the great freedom of not having ways or forms.

She wasn't fooling herself: was it possible that those perfect moments would pass? Leaving her in the middle of an unknown path? But she could always keep in her hands a bit of what she was getting to know now, and then it would be easier to live not living, barely living. Even if she were never again to feel the serious and serene power of existing and loving, as she did now, in the future she would already know what to wait for, waiting her whole life if necessary, and if necessary never again having what she was waiting for. She suddenly shifted in bed because it was unbearable to imagine for an instant that she might never repeat her profound existence on earth. But, to her unexpected joy, she realized she'd always love him. After Ulisses had become hers, being human now seemed to her the right way of being a living animal. And through Ulisses's great love, she finally understood the kind of beauty she had. It was a beauty that nothing and no one could reach and take away, because it was so high, big, deep, and dark. As if her image were reflected trembling in a reservoir of black and translucent waters.

Sleep would sometimes come to her but she was afraid to wake up, be again the former woman. The precariousness of the true life inside her was devastating. She reached out her arm in the dark and in the dark her hand touched the naked chest of the sleeping man: she was creating him by her own hand and making sure her hand would forever carry the imprint of life on its skin. "God," she thought, "so this is what you seemed to be promising me." And her eyes closed in a semisleep, in a semivigil, for she was keeping vigil over the sleep of her great love.

It was in this dream-glimmer state that she dreamt seeing that the fruit of the world was hers. Or if it wasn't, that she'd just touched it. It was an enormous, scarlet, and heavy fruit that was hanging in the dark space, shining with an almost golden light. And that right in the air itself she was placing her mouth on the fruit and managing to bite it, leaving it nevertheless whole, glistening in space. For that's how it was with Ulisses: they had possessed each other more than seemed possible and permitted, and nevertheless he and she were whole. The fruit was whole, yes, though in her mouth she felt as a living thing the food of the land. It was holy land because it was the only one on which a human could say while loving: I am yours and you are mine, and we is one.

Until Lóri fell asleep more deeply and the darkness was all hers.

After a little while they awoke and both Ulisses and Lóri reached a hand out to the other's hand.

—My love, she said.

—Yes?

But she didn't reply. Then he said:

—We both know we're at the threshold of a door open to a new life. It's the door, Lóri. And we know that only the death of one of us will separate us. No, Lóri, it won't be an easy life. But it's a new life. (Everything seems like a dream to me. But it's not, he said, reality is what's unbelievable.)

Ulisses, wise Ulisses, had lost his tranquility upon finding love for the first time in his life. His voice was different, it had lost its professorial tone, his voice now was that of just a man.

Had he wanted to teach Lóri through formulae? No, for he wasn't a man of formulae, since no formula would do: he was lost in a sea of joy and of the menace of pain. Lóri could finally speak to him as an equal. Because finally he was realizing that he didn't know anything and the weight was making his voice catch. But he wanted the dangerous new life.

—I always had to fight my tendency to be the servant of a man, Lóri said, so deeply did I admire men compared to women. In men I feel the courage to be alive. Whereas I, woman, am a bit more refined and for that very reason weaker—you are primitive and direct.

—Lóri, you are now a super-woman in the sense that I'm a super-man, just because we have the courage to go through the open door. It's down to us whether we manage painstakingly to be what we really are. We, like all people, have the potential to be gods. I don't mean gods in the divine sense. First we must follow nature, not forgetting its low moments, since nature is cyclical, it's rhythm, it's like a beating heart. Existing is so completely out of the ordinary that if we were aware of existing for more than a few seconds, we'd go mad. The solution to this absurdity called "I exist," the solution is to love another being who, this someone else, we understand does exist.

—My love, she said smiling, you seduced me diabolically. Without sadness or regret, I feel as if I've finally bitten the flesh of the fruit I thought was forbidden. You transformed me into the woman I am. You seduced me, she smiled. But there's no dirtiness inside me. I am pure like a woman in bed with a man. A woman is never pornographic. I wouldn't know how to be, though I've never been as intimately with anyone. Do you understand?

—I understand and know that. But I don't like to say everything. You too should learn to keep silent so you don't get lost in words.

—No. I kept silent all my life. But all right, I'll say less. What I'd like to know is whether in your eyes I'm the unfortunate heroine who sheds her clothes. I'm naked in body and soul, but I want the darkness to wrap around me and cover me, no, don't turn on the light.

—Yes.

Ulisses had previously lacked a certain humility. But in love, out of awe, he had become humble and serene.

—I love you, Lóri, and I don't have much time for you because I work a lot. It was always an effort to find time to have a whiskey with you. I'm going to have more work, you'll have to be patient, more work because I finally have to write my essay. And I'll write without any style, he said as if talking to himself. Writing without style is the most anyone who writes can desire. It will be, Lóri, like that thing you said which I memorized: it will be the world with its haughty impersonality versus my individuality as a person but we shall be one. You'll often have to be alone.

—I don't mind. I'm a different woman now. And a minute of certainty about your love will last me for weeks, I'm a different woman. And I even want to be busier: teaching is becoming a passion, I want to clothe, and teach, and love my students, and prepare them in a way I was never prepared.

—You're the same as you ever were. You've just bloomed into a blood-red rose. I threw away the two dozen roses because I have you, a big rose and with moist and thick petals. Lóri, I'm going to be so busy that we might need to get married in order to be together.

—Maybe that would be better. Maybe it's best to—

He interrupted her kissing lingeringly her scented flesh. And she again fell into the vertigo that overtook her, and again was happy the way a being can die of happiness. And again for the fourth time they loved each other.

Afterward he asked if she minded if he turned on the lights because he wanted to see her. She said he could. Then they looked at each other. Both were pale and both thought they were beautiful. She covered her body with the sheet. Soon they were smoking with cigarettes in one hand and with the other holding hands. For a long time they sat in silence. Even Lóri wasn't following her own thoughts until she reached somewhat unexpectedly the sudden question:

—What is my social value, Ulisses? These days, I mean.

—That of a woman who isn't integrated into the Brazilian society of today, into its bourgeois middle class.

—As I see it, you don't belong to any class, Ulisses. If you only knew how exciting it is for me to imitate you. I learn from you but you think that I learned from your lessons, yet that wasn't it, I learned something you weren't even dreaming of teaching me. Do you think I'm offending my social structure with my great freedom?

—Of course you do, thankfully. Because you're leaving prison as a free being, and no one will forgive you that. Sex and love aren't forbidden for you. You finally learned to exist. And that unlocks many other freedoms, which is a risk to your society. Even the freedom to be good to yourself frightens others. You'll see how much better you'll teach. But the two of us, if we have a child, we're ready.

—I'd have liked to get pregnant tonight.

—Be patient. Anyway, next time, you should be careful because we'll wait for the right moment to have a child. First, not least to make that easier, we really should marry.

She got up wrapped in the sheet and turned off the lights. There was already a predawn shade. And the even darker shade, since they'd seen each other, was good to them. They sat in silence for so long that for an instant, in the moment of greatest darkness that precedes the dawn, she didn't realize where she was. There was such a wonderful chaos and nebula that she squeezed his hand so that someone could keep her on earth. They remained silent and let go of each other's hands and stubbed out their cigarettes. She no longer felt the jealousy she'd felt when she entered the bedroom and noticed that he had a double bed, with two bedside tables and two ashtrays. Now she'd never be jealous again.

Minutes later she said:

—I still find no answer when I ask: who am I? But I think I now know: profoundly I am the one who has her own life and also your life. I drank our life.

—But you can't ask that. And the question should have a different answer. Don't pretend you're strong enough to ask a human being's worst question. I, who am stronger than you, can't ask myself "who am I" without getting lost.

And his voice had sounded like that of someone lost.

She wasn't startled when she felt his hand rest on her stomach. The hand was now caressing her legs. In that moment there was no sensuality between them. Though she was full of wonders, as if full of stars. She then reached out her own hand and touched his sex which was immediately transformed: but he stayed quiet. They both seemed calm and a little sad.

—Could love be giving your own solitude to another? Because that's the ultimate thing you can give of yourself, said Ulisses.

—I don't know, my love, but I know that my path has reached its end: I mean I reached the door of a beginning.

—Woman of mine, he said.

—Yes, Lóri said, I am your woman.

Dawn was opening in faltering light. For Lóri the atmosphere was miraculous. She had reached the impossible of herself. Then she said, because she was feeling that Ulisses was once again caught by the pain of existing:

—My love, you don't believe in the God because we erred by humanizing him. We humanized Him because we didn't understand Him, so it didn't work. I'm sure He isn't human. But though not human, nonetheless He still sometimes makes us divine. Do you think that—

—I think, the man interrupted and his voice was slow and muffled because he was suffering from life and from love, this is what I think:

Afterword

A HUMAN BEING IS A CREATURE WHO IS LOST, WHO IS
singular, who merges with and is like everything in existence,
who knows and doesn't know God, who has been steeped in
pain and who is afraid to love and wants to love and be loved
by another person more than anything else in the world. That
is the quest of this book: to love and be loved. But in order to
truly love and be loved, one must first find one's way to the
most difficult thing, which is a joyful relationship "with the
mightiness of life." And while most love stories do away with
this requirement and don't even recognize it—just have the
lovers hurtling toward each other—this love story is a question about this requirement, and can it even be won?

Who is this man, this Ulisses, who asks of Lóri that she
become somehow different before they come together in love?
Who is this Lóri, who accepts this demand, and sets off down
the road toward it? Who are these bizarre creatures, who ask
of each other what no two people who are suffering from desire have perhaps ever asked of the other one?

How does Ulisses know that Lóri hasn't yet become the full
expression of herself? How does he know that she is someone

who exists only through pain and suffering, and not through gladness and joy? How does he know, right from the start, that she "wasn't up to enjoying a man"?

We are brought into the story only after all this knowledge has been won.

* * *

Before I start reading a book by Clarice Lispector, I always go off somewhere I can be alone, and I don't check my phone or do anything else until the final page. I prefer to read her from start to finish, without interruption. Her novels are something I want to undergo, like a spiritual exercise. Just as Lóri both loses and finds herself in the salty sea with its "unlimited cold that without rage roars," I feel, when reading her books, as if I am submerged in just as deep a vastness, in the great soul of a great writer who has access to all of Nature unvarnished. I feel "a dizzying seasickness that stirs [me] from the sleep of ages," wakened by her philosophical mind, which seems to have grasped the deepest structure and meaning of the greatest mysteries of life. Yet twinned with her esoteric knowledge is also so much insecurity and doubt. This at first feels surprising—then it does not. In fact, it comes to seem outrageous that we had not known all along that of course the wisest among us would also worry about how to enter a party without exposing how vulnerable she feels.

As spiritually profound as her writings are, they are also sensually grounded in the things of the world and the pettiest aspects of life as a human—and as a woman specifically. But that all these things are important to the same mind makes the pettinesses seem profound, or at least inseparable from our lives here on earth.

***

True love involves waiting for one's love is something we might guess from all the world's love stories, but I have never before seen the trial of this waiting so transparently formulated as a spiritual discipline through which one comes to win that love and deserve it.

Each of the two lovers in *An Apprenticeship* holds all of the power, and each holds none. Each has total dominion over the other, and each is completely flattened beneath the other one's heel. Although we only see the affair from Lóri's perspective, it is easy enough to suffer alongside Ulisses, when Lóri doesn't show up to their meetings, or even touch his hand.

In reading Lispector's books, I learn about the structure of the relationship between a human and God, between a human and herself, and between a human and the other; in this case, both the other who is just another person one has slept with and lost desire for, and the Other who holds your life's happiness in their hands. This second Other is the elemental force that drives the life of the loving one, while the other other has no power at all and might as well not even exist. Why is life like this? How can so much importance (for the one who loves) be concentrated in a random, Other, singular individual, while diffused among the rest is nothing, and we are able to stride past them with complete indifference?

What is this Other capable of that the other other could never do? In one sense (unhappy as this is to write) the Other is the one who circumscribes our limits. With the choice of who to love, we end up in a city, with a side of the bed on which to sleep, and a certain set of friends (growing further apart from those who are not invited over because one's partner does not like them). We watch certain shows, not others. And the Other circumscribes our limits metaphysically, too. Maybe this procedure is necessary, in order for our lives to have a form. Just as the art-impulse must take a certain form—a sculpture, a play, a novel, a dance—so does the election of a specific Other shape our blobbish life-impulse into a specific form. I am now thinking of the part of the novel where Clarice writes, "Lóri had a kind of dread of going, as if she could go too far—in what direction? Which was making it hard to go … There was a certain fear of her own capacity, large or small, maybe because she didn't know her own limits. Were the limits of a human divine? They were."

And so we choose a man or woman to confer some needed limits.

In this book, both Lóri and Ulisses "are attractive as man and woman." He is a man with whom women easily fall in love, and she is a woman who surpasses everyone in the room, "in educational skills, in intuitive understanding, and even in feminine charm." Their magnetism is a gift from the gods: she is that rare woman "who hasn't broken from the lineage of women down through time," and he, "from the viewpoint of strictly masculine beauty [had] a calm virility inside him." She knows what she is doing in bed—you only have to glance at her to see it. And he has the ability to seduce. It's like any Hollywood movie: the leading man must be attractive, and so must the leading lady, so we understand why she desires him (because we do too), and why he desires her (because we do too). And so Lispector makes them both desirable—or tells us that they are. (Because of course Ulisses is not! I mean, he has the manly virtue of self-restraint, but apart from that, what? Wouldn't I throw down my napkin in disgust onto the elegant tablecloth of the restaurant we were sitting in if he spoke to me as he does her?—but he wouldn't want me.)

So what locks her in?

Lóri has the twinned feminine virtue and vice of radical self-doubt (which perhaps I also have—but in life, not while reading a book), which makes one susceptible to other people, sometimes to a dangerous degree. That Ulisses resists her sexual charms seems to be all she needs to know that he's the one to whom she must surrender. He can resist her, so he must be above her. And because she is below him, she is ready to make him her teacher. What does he hope to teach her? How to be worthy of him. Which is also how to be worthy of life itself— to be like rain, "without gratitude or ingratitude."

This is an incredibly difficult task. It takes great deal of patience to bring herself to that place, and she undergoes a lot of suffering—but also gains more illumination than many people find in a lifetime. Isn't it horrible? What a plot! Yet can I say Lispector is wrong? It is always tempting to try to make oneself worthy of those who have put themselves above you (or who you have put above you), and nothing is more humiliating than to fail to perform this task well. Anyway, it is a story that should be told.

(I have also tried to look at waiting for love as a spiritual discipline, from even its smallest expression: like trying not to destroy myself in agony over the pain of being a human who knows she has sent a bad email to someone she admires, from whom she believes she won't—and actually doesn't— hear back. That feeling is just a speck of what Clarice Lispector is writing about here, as one of the most important things we grapple with: how to assure ourselves that we are—and to actually be—worthy of loving and being loved.)

All love stories must have their obstacles: religion, parents, a stone wall. The obstacle in this book is that we may be unfit for love, plain and simple: because we haven't lived in such a way that we have let ourselves be fit for it; we haven't even lived in such a way that we have made ourselves fit for life. For God. For sex. For anything! We slack off on the spiritual level, always. We guess no one's going to see it. Who's looking? Even we are not. Then someone like Ulisses comes along and says, *You cannot have me until you do the difficult work of being a human that you have been putting off.* (And inwardly, the man says to himself, *I am also not worthy of her, and cannot have her until I make myself fit for love, too.*)

Is this book a fantasy, in a way? While some writers might fantasize about a man coming along who will shower a woman in diamonds and install her in a penthouse, Clarice Lispector, the great mystic, spins a fantasy of having an explicit reason for doing the most difficult labor a person is capable of: the work of becoming an actual human being in this world. Here, the motive to do the work is to win the love of a man. (But a man is not just some guy; he represents one of the elemental forces of the universe—the masculine force that sets the difficult task in motion, of impelling the feminine force, which would otherwise sit, roundly, alone. What woman has not felt that unfortunate thing, that some man, not yet won, was "like the border between the past and whatever was to come"? Yet in a way, isn't Ulisses asking Lóri to find the masculine force within herself, before coming to him? Or to find it in herself so she doesn't come to him seeking it, then get bored of what she's found, like any woman who goes from man to man, never satisfied because she's mistaken about what she is looking for, really? Yes. Any woman wanting any sort of lasting happiness has to realize that she can — and must — be the impelling force that moves herself through the world.)

The end point of all this spiritual labor isn't a lasting happiness. Then what *is* the prize of the work of becoming human (work that those worthy of our love make us twist ourselves up in order to achieve — or else never achieve, which they will never cease to remind us of)? Is the prize simply a few private moments between ourselves and the universe, which are so magnificent — moments of true grace — such as Lóri encounters on the way to her man? Or is the prize of all that spiritual effort just hearing, and being able to honestly say, *I love you*? Is it a marriage in which one's spouse is going to be working on a long essay, leaving one alone a lot? Or is the prize being interrupted midsentence by the person one loves, in bed? The struggle toward love is presented as an apprenticeship — but an apprenticeship in what? An ordinary kind of marriage? And after an apprenticeship, we supposedly become masters — but of what? Loving? Living?

No, never masters, for the master understands her craft — whether it's an art form, or the craft of life, or of love — while the apprentice does not. As Lispector writes, "not-understanding" would always be better than "understanding," for not-understanding "had no frontiers and led to the infinite, to the God." Lóri, Ulisses, we, Clarice, remain apprentices, always — apprentices in everything — because apprentices feel more, think more, struggle more, and win more than the master, who has already arrived, ever can.

SHEILA HETI